BRAD'S RETURN

Lee worked for Mrs Palmerston and her son, Phillip, who ran the family estate. The other son, Brad, was rarely mentioned, but when Mrs Palmerston was taken ill, Lee wrote to let him know. When Brad returned, Phillip showed an interest in Lee he had never shown before and accused her of favouring Brad. Lee was afraid to accept Brad's friendship, especially when she was told that he would use any girl and then drop her. Yet she couldn't help loving him.

Books by Hilda Durman
in the Linford Romance Library:

HILDA DURMAN

BRAD'S RETURN

Complete and Unabridged

LINFORD
Leicester

First published in Great Britain in 1982

First Linford Edition
published 2000

British Library CIP Data

Durman, Hilda
    Brad's return.—Large print ed.—
Linford romance library
    1. Love stories
    2. Large type books
    I. Title
    823.9′14 [F]

ISBN 0–7089–5748–X

Published by
F. A. Thorpe (Publishing)
Anstey, Leicestershire

Set by Words & Graphics Ltd.
Anstey, Leicestershire
Printed and bound in Great Britain by
T. J. International Ltd., Padstow, Cornwall

This book is printed on acid-free paper

1

Lee Robson had been working for the Palmerston family for nearly two years now and in all that time she had rarely heard them mention Brad, the eldest son. He was somewhere the other side of the world, she gathered, and from snatches of conversation she had overheard it seemed he was considered the black sheep of the family.

Phillip, his younger brother, had helped his father on the estate and he had been his father's blue-eyed boy. He could do no wrong in his father's estimation. Mr Palmerston had died nearly a year ago and Phillip was carrying on on his own now and Brad hadn't even come home for the funeral.

Mrs Palmerston was a very reserved lady and if she grieved over the absence of her eldest son she didn't show it. Lee

1

had come to do some typing for her when she was writing a book on local history and helped her a lot with the research, and somehow she had fitted into the family routine and her services had been sought continually from that time. Mrs Palmerston had suggested that she move in with them to save journeys backwards and forwards to her own home. Sometimes Lee found herself typing for Mrs Palmerston, but sometimes she was also acting as part-time secretary for Mr Palmerston and his son. In addition she helped Mrs Palmerston with her numerous committees and charity work. Lee was very versatile and there were not many jobs she couldn't tackle. She often referred to herself as a general dog's body. Her salary was good but she earned every penny she received.

Lee liked her job and loved living in the Palmerstons' house which was like a small mansion set in the midst of parkland. Her family often felt she was making a mistake being buried alive, as they called it, in the country, not meeting people of her own class and spoiling her chances of meeting a nice young fellow with whom to settle down in married bliss.

Sometimes Phillip took her out and she met his friends, but although his friends made her welcome, she was always more or less kept in her place. Her background did not fit in with Phillip's wealthy friends, or so she imagined. Lee didn't mind. She never tried to appear other than she was, a working girl from an ordinary working-class family. She had no doubt that if she suddenly came into a fortune, or discovered that she had aristocratic ancestors, she would have been accepted as one of the élite, but she didn't particularly want to be.

She didn't mind being an onlooker. She loved to see how the wealthy lived, but was not always keen on the wealthy themselves. She had her own little Mini and could drive over to her home quite frequently so as not to be out of touch with her own people.

It was when Mrs Palmerston fainted for no reason at all one day that Lee suggested to Phillip that perhaps Brad should know about it. She knew he hadn't come home for his father's funeral, but it had been too late for him to come and see him then. Perhaps he would want to be informed that his mother had been ill. The doctor had been worried about her fainting, and yet he said he couldn't find a reason for it. Her heart was in good condition, but nevertheless she had been out for quite a time before they had been able to bring her round. Mrs Palmerston herself worried over it and said she hoped it didn't happen again.

At first Phillip seemed angry at her suggestion that she should let Brad know of his mother's blackout.

'He doesn't care about her,' he said. 'He would have come over when Dad died if he cared about her. He must have known how shattered she'd be by Dad's death, but it didn't bring him home to comfort her.'

Lee could see that Phillip hated his brother and she wondered why.

'Well, at least you would have nothing on your conscience if you'd notified him that your mother had fainted for no reason and you thought he ought to know,' she suggested.

'You can write and tell him if you like. Mother writes to him but I don't suppose she'll mention anything to upset him. I'll get you the address,' he said, grudgingly. He obviously didn't intend to write himself.

The letter Lee wrote to Brad was very short. She said he wouldn't know who she was and explained that she had been working for his mother for nearly two years now and she thought he should know that his mother had had a blackout although the doctor hadn't given them any cause for alarm.

She saw that the address given to her was Rio de Janeiro, and she tried to remember all that she had read and heard about Rio. The letter went by air mail and then she put it out of her mind. Why Brad Palmerston didn't come home was nothing to do with her. She only knew it seemed the right thing to do to let him know about his mother.

Shortly afterwards, Mrs Palmerston received a letter from him. Her face had flushed when she read the letter which Lee had seen in the morning mail and guessed it was from Brad. Lee couldn't be sure whether his mother was pleased or annoyed. 'A letter from Brad,' she announced, as they were at the breakfast table.

Phillip looked across at Lee, knowing she had written to him as she had said she would, but he didn't mention that fact.

'What's he say?' he asked, without showing any interest.

'He's coming to England quite soon and will be coming to see us.'

'Will he be coming on his own?'

'He doesn't say,' said his mother.

Phillip rose from the table and went

outside and his mother looked after him anxiously, then she turned to Lee.

'Perhaps you wonder about my eldest son, Brad? You must feel that it's strange that he hasn't been home for so long. I'm afraid that I'm very much to blame myself. You see he and his father used to have some terrible quarrels and I felt I couldn't stand it so I told him to clear off and leave us alone.'

'And he did?'

'Yes. But I didn't expect him to leave the country. At first it was a relief that he wasn't here to worry his father. I worried in case his father should have a stroke when he used to get into such tempers, yet after Brad had been gone for some time I had the feeling his father missed him as much as I did.'

'I suppose you told him to clear off in anger and regretted it afterwards?'

'No, I wasn't angry. Perhaps he wouldn't have taken me seriously if I had been. I was in deadly earnest.

He and his father were always at loggerheads and I felt I couldn't stand it any more. He was always a rebel and when he was older he and his father clashed over the running of the estate. They had different temperaments and could never agree on anything. I told Brad to go and leave us in peace.'

It was nothing to do with Lee so she couldn't comment, but she did feel it a bit drastic to tell a son to clear off because he and his father didn't see eye to eye. Mrs Palmerston was sitting quietly as if thinking back over the years.

'There were other things, too,' she said. 'I never dreamt that Brad could behave as he did.'

'And now he's coming to see you,' said Lee. 'Perhaps he's changed now he's older.'

'Maybe, but I can't imagine Brad being any different. He has very strong opinions of his own. It's been over two years since he went away. He was thirty then and his father had relied on him to run the estate in his later years.'

'He had Phillip,' said Lee.

'Yes, he had Phillip, but a father looks to his eldest son to carry on after him. Brad should have taken the burden from him but he wasn't there to do it, and Phillip, although Brad and his father never agreed, was second best.'

That seemed strange to Lee. Why, if Brad was supposed to be such a difficult person, quarrelling with his father and those other things hinted at besides, should Mr Palmerston have been disappointed that Phillip had been there to work with him instead of Brad? As far as Lee could see, Phillip was running everything to the best of his ability since his father died.

Phillip was obviously not overjoyed at the thought of his brother's return. Perhaps he anticipated trouble when the black sheep came home.

Lee carried on with her work as usual and couldn't help wondering whether it would be long before Brad put in an appearance and tried to imagine what he was like.

She was to find out sooner than she expected. Since coming to work at the home of the Palmerstons she had learned to ride a horse, something she had never had the opportunity to do before, and most mornings she was up early in order to have a canter over the fields, a lovely way to start a day.

She was often accompanied by Phillip who was never more than just friendly with her. She couldn't imagine him being anything more than friendly, nor did she desire him to be. They had set out on this particular spring morning, admiring the hosts of daffodils and early tulips forcing their way through, as they made their way towards the open countryside where the hedges and trees were beginning to give signs of new greenery. They had been returning together, making their way over the cobbled yard towards the stables when they saw the luxurious car parked before the house. She heard Phillip murmur,

'Brad!' as the man got out of the car.

He was nothing like Phillip. Lee wouldn't have taken them for brothers. Phillip was almost sandy-haired, fair of skin with blue eyes, but his brother was extremely dark and he was very tanned due to his prolonged stay in Brazil.

He came towards them eyeing them intently. There was no sign of a smile on his face or Phillip's and Lee felt this was a strange homecoming for someone who had been away so long.

Brad waited for them to dismount before coming quite close to them. 'Just arrived?' asked Phillip.

'This very minute,' said Brad, looking at Lee and waiting to be introduced.

'Miss Lee Robson,' said Phillip, 'Mother's secretary cum assistant, cum everything, I suppose. Lee this is my brother Brad, as you've no doubt guessed.'

'Yes. How do you do?' she said, offering her hand.

He took it briefly and she found herself looking into a pair of deep blue eyes, a far deeper blue than Phillip's. As soon as he released her hand she made her excuses and left the two brothers together.

He was a very handsome man, she decided. But of course looks were nothing to go by. His features were well cut and he had rather a severe look about him when he took her hand. He didn't have the type of looks one would associate with the black sheep of the family. There seemed strength in his face rather than weakness. And of course that marvellous tan made him look so much more handsome. It surprised her that she had taken in so much about him from that short meeting. She hoped his mother would be pleased to see him. She was bound to be. Lee couldn't imagine a mother not wanting to be on speaking terms with a son like that. He seemed the type any mother would be proud to acknowledge as her son.

She rushed upstairs and changed out of her riding habit into her everyday wear and to her own surprise found herself taking extra special care when she brushed her hair and attended to her light make-up before going downstairs.

Lee didn't need the help of make-up to make her look beautiful. She had that young fresh look; cheeks that were pink without too much colour, eyes that sparkled when she was animated and could look solemn and serious, too. Her hair was like a dark cap of sheer silk which she wore with a fringe and the not too long ends turned under. When she tossed her head it moved altogether and then settled back into place again. She was very slim having been a dancing fanatic when she was a child, studying tap, ballet and modern dancing so that she moved with the grace of a dancer. Her hands were well shaped and slim, but quite capable of doing all sorts of work. There wasn't a lazy bone in Lee's body.

She was a little apprehensive about

going down to breakfast now that Brad had arrived. Perhaps Phillip and his mother would want to talk to him in private. But Lee was hungry after her horse-riding and decided she would slip into the kitchen for something to eat if she felt her presence would be embarrassing to them this morning.

But when she got downstairs Mrs Palmerston heard her going towards the kitchen and called her into the dining-room where she was sitting at the table with her two sons. 'We've been waiting for you,' said Phillip.

'Sorry,' she said. 'I thought you might like to talk to Brad on your own as he's only just arrived.'

'I don't know why you should think that,' said Brad, drily. 'I gathered you were almost one of the family.'

Lee felt confused looking from Phillip to his mother and wondering what had been said about her. She took her place at the table after helping herself to coffee and noticed that Brad's mother could hardly take her eyes off him and hung on to every word he said. There was no doubt at all that she idolised this handsome son of hers and Lee felt angry with him for causing her distress as he had obviously done in the past.

He was telling them that he was due for a holiday and had left his affairs in South America in good hands. 'How would you like to come to Brazil with me, Mother, for a long holiday?' he asked. 'You'd like it.'

'Oh, I'd be like a fish out of water if I left this place,' she said.

'Go on with you. A holiday would do you good. Phillip doesn't need you to help with the estate, does he?'

'I have so many other commitments,' she said.

'You would soon pick up the threads again when you returned,' countered Brad. 'I'd like you to come and see where I live.'

'Haven't you missed your home in England?' she asked.

His keen blue eyes met hers. 'What do you think?' he asked her.

His mother looked away and Lee remembered that Mrs Palmerston had told her that she had told Brad to clear off and leave them in peace.

'I'm completely shattered after my flight,' he said, when breakfast was almost over. 'I don't know whether I'm coming or going. I think a few hours' sleep is first priority.'

Lee noticed that Phillip had very little to say to his brother though Brad, having done most of the talking, directed his conversation to all three of them.

Perhaps it was tiredness that gave Brad that grim look about his mouth at times, thought Lee, when he went off to get that sleep he had promised himself. When he had gone she wondered which one, Phillip or his mother, had told Brad that she was almost one of the family.

Lee went off to the study to carry on with the accounts for Phillip. She kept all the ledgers in order so that the accountant's work was easy when he came to look through them. She knew that the expense of running the estate these days was astronomical and that the income from various sources very often was not sufficient to cover overheads and that this caused great anxiety to Mrs Palmerston, and probably to Phillip, too, though he didn't seem to worry as much as his mother did. Phillip said that their troubles were due to the recession, that everyone was having a difficult time these days to keep their heads above water, but Lee often wondered how long the Palmerstons could carry on subsidising the estate from their own capital.

Phillip came into the study and sat himself down which was a rare event. He was content to let her get on with the work without taking a terrific lot of interest in how she was getting on with it. There had never been any complaints from the accountants and he admitted that he hadn't much idea himself about the financial running of the estate. He worked mainly out of doors supervising the work of the men employed by him.

Lee noticed that Phillip was looking at her with more than usual interest. She knew that he had never regarded her in any other light than that of his mother's secretary who was now his as well, and that she was a useful person to have around, being at the beck and call of his mother at all times. Not that Lee felt put on, for Mrs Palmerston was not a slave driver, and if Lee wanted a few days off to visit her family, or an hour or two to go to town she never felt afraid to ask for her employer would agree quite readily to her having a break.

'What did you think about my brother?' asked Phillip.

Lee put her pen down and looked towards him. 'He's very handsome,' she smiled. 'Far better looking than I expected.'

Phillip scowled. 'You mean he puts me in the shade?'

'Oh, no,' Lee protested. 'I didn't mean anything like that at all. I daresay if you were tanned like Brad you'd look extremely handsome, too. It's surprising what a tan does for a person.'

'There's no need to pretend,' said Phillip, bitterly. 'I know that Brad always puts me in the shade. And of course, with his looks, the women flock after him. And he has no scruples. He'll take any man's girl.'

Lee looked at Phillip curiously. He had never spoken confidentially to her before. 'Are you trying to tell me that Brad has stolen girl friends from you?' she smiled. 'That's not unusual in families. When I've taken boy friends home my sisters have tried to steal them from me. If they can be stolen their love wasn't very strong in the first place.'

'But they wouldn't try to take a fellow from you if they knew you really cared about him?'

'I suppose not,' said Lee.

'Well, that's what Brad did to me.

Took the only girl I really wanted to marry.'

Lee looked at him sympathetically. 'Perhaps he didn't realise you cared that much. Did he marry her?'

'No. He took her abroad with him but then I heard she'd married someone else.'

'So the tables were turned on Brad,' said Lee. 'That should give you some satisfaction. And you've had time to get over it now, haven't you?'

'It takes a long time to get over something like that,' said Phillip. 'I just thought I'd put you on your guard. For some reason Brad got the impression that you were important to me seeing us both together this morning, and that's a challenge to him. He'll try to get you for himself.'

'But you can soon put him wise. You can let him know that I mean nothing at all except a good secretary, I hope,' she smiled.

'I don't know,' said Phillip. 'Since Brad has arrived and I noticed at the breakfast table that he had his eyes on you I found I disliked intensely the idea of his getting his hands on you.'

'Oh, Phillip! I've only seen him for a very short time and I'm hardly likely to give him the opportunity to get his hands on me, as you put it, after such a short acquaintance.'

'He'll start to work on you. Every pretty girl is a challenge to him.'

Lee found the idea a little exciting. Being chased by Brad wouldn't be bad at all. 'I can look after myself,' she said. 'I can tell when a man is sincere and when he isn't. You don't reach the age of twenty-three without knowing something about men.'

'You wouldn't let him draw you away from me, Lee?' asked Phillip.

She looked at him in surprise. She only worked for him. What difference did it make to him whether she was drawn to his brother or any other man, for that matter? He could always get himself another secretary.

'You mean he might ask me to do

some work for him?' she asked. 'I would have to see if I could fit it in, of course. Naturally you and your mother have first priority.'

'You are deliberately misunderstanding me,' he said. 'I'm not talking about work. I'm talking about Brad trying to win your affection from me.'

Lee looked at him incredulously. 'I've never given you any cause to believe that I regard you as anything other than my employer, surely?' she said, not in a tone of annoyance, but of surprise. Phillip couldn't possibly imagine that she had ever shown anything different in their relationship from an employee and an employer. Even when he took her out sometimes she was always conscious of that.

'After working for us for so long I can't believe that you don't have some deeper feeling towards me than that of a secretary towards her boss.'

'Honestly, Phillip,' she said, her eyes looking wide and anxious, 'I have never regarded you as anything but my employer. It would have been embarrassing for you if I had shown any deeper feeling.'

'Supposing I told you I would like you to feel special to me?'

Lee felt uncomfortable, and she suspected that the only reason why Phillip was talking like this was because Brad was here now and he feared he might try to steal his secretary. Was it because he would hate his brother to steal her away, or was he genuinely concerned that Brad might hurt her? She didn't know where to look, finding that she couldn't meet his eyes. 'You don't really want me to feel special to you,' she said. 'It's just something that has occurred to you because you feel you might be in competition with your brother. Well, I can assure you that I shall bear in mind what you've said about Brad and shall take everything he says with a pinch of salt.'

'But I hope you won't take everything I say with a pinch of salt, Lee. I want you to consider what I have said very seriously. I'll take you out more and we'll get to know each other better. Not working together, but enjoying life together.'

Lee laughed. She didn't know how else to react. She felt she knew Phillip as well as she would ever do and he had never set her pulses racing. As an employer he was nice enough, but he definitely wasn't her type of man, she was sure of that.

Phillip was annoyed with her for laughing at him. She didn't want to hurt his feelings and said, 'I'm not laughing at you, Phillip, but at the thought of your suggestion.'

'Why should it be amusing?'

'I'm sure you've never given it a minute's thought before about taking me out and getting to know me. You've had plenty of opportunities if you had wanted to know me better but it's just because Brad's back, isn't it? You think he's going to change everything. But he won't be here for long. He's only on a holiday. It has made his mother happy to see him again. He knows about her blackout and has seen for himself that she seems to have got over it okay. He'll be gone soon and everything will be back to normal. You'll see.'

But Phillip wouldn't be put off. She hadn't realised he had this stubborn streak in him. 'I'm going to take you out as often as I can,' he declared.

'Please remember, Phillip, that I couldn't possibly dress in the style that your friends do and it would be embarrassing for me to have to meet people you know knowing that I am not wearing clothes up to their standard.'

'I'll attend to that.'

'You mean you'd buy clothes for me! Oh, no Phillip. I have my pride, you know. I should hate to have to think that you had to buy clothes for me in order that I could seem to be in the same class as people you associate with.'

'I've never noticed anything wrong with the clothes you wear,' he said, angrily.

'That's because you're a man. Women are supposed to dress to please their men, but they dress more to impress their lady friends. Most men wouldn't know whether an outfit cost the earth or not, but women know.'

'You're putting stupid obstacles in the way, Lee. Supposing I asked you to marry me? Would you object to my buying clothes for you then?'

'No. It would be different if you were my husband, but you're not likely to propose to me, Phillip, and if you did I wouldn't accept and I don't mean that unkindly.'

'I've taken you unawares,' he said, rising from his chair. 'But I want you to think things over, Lee.'

She didn't answer and he repeated. 'I seriously want you to think it over, Lee. Promise me you will?'

'I'll certainly think about what you've said,' she told him, not wishing to seem ungrateful for his offer, but knowing full well that his suggestion that they should get to know each other more didn't appeal to her at all. She felt quite certain that he had had no interest in her until he got the idea that Brad might take an interest in her. He was like a child with a toy. He didn't want to play with it himself until he saw that someone else wanted it. And Phillip was afraid that Brad might take to her, show an interest in her and he didn't intend to allow him to do so. He was trying to stake his claim to her first and Lee knew that he had no claim on her at all.

She hoped that Brad's visit would be short and sweet and was sure that when he left, Phillip would give up all ideas of wanting to know his secretary better, and would be thankful that she had not taken him up on the offer for she had no intention of falling in with his suggestions.

2

A smile played around Lee's mouth as she picked up her Biro and continued to enter figures into the ledgers. The idea of becoming special to Phillip Palmerston was absolutely ludicrous. Perhaps if Brad's stay at home was only to be a short one she should ask for a few weeks off. Say that she'd decided to have her holidays early this year and then Phillip would not feel apprehensive about her and Brad.

She found herself wondering about Brad. He was a very handsome man and somehow she couldn't imagine that he would have to stoop to stealing his brother's girl friends. He was surely quite capable of taking his pick from any number of girls. She had found him a very attractive male. Yet she supposed there were some men who got a kick out of stealing a girl from someone else and then they found they didn't want them. Perhaps that was what had happened when he had stolen Phillip's girl, taking her with him a couple of years ago. Once he'd got her he didn't want her. Or, perhaps the girl had discovered that he wasn't a good catch after all if she'd married someone else. It was strange that Brad had gone so far as to take the girl to Brazil with him.

She finished off her work on the ledgers and went in search of Mrs Palmerston to see what jobs she required doing.

'I've a list of items I'd like you to get for me here,' said her employer. They kept a book specially for entering items which they required because they were a distance from the shops and it was most annoying to return from town finding that something essential had been overlooked.

Lee had lunch first and then started out in her Mini for the nearest town which was five miles away. There were little shops in the villages between the estate and the town, but there was a greater selection in the larger shops.

When she had finished her shopping Lee made a quick dash to her home to see her parents and other members of her family who might be assembled there. She was lucky today. Both her parents were in and a couple of her sisters, Jane and Catherine, both younger than herself. She enjoyed a cup of coffee with them and a chat before having to start back to the Palmerstons' home.

She found herself talking about Brad who had returned from abroad after such a long time. 'I believe he's been a bit of a lad in his day,' said Lee, without malice because she didn't know a great deal about him. 'But he's certainly dishy.'

She was surprised at her own enthusiasm in describing Brad and remembered that Phillip had warned her not to let him use his charm on her. It seemed that she had been affected by his presence without his having used one iota of energy in exerting his charms. His mere presence had been enough to excite her.

'It's no use getting ideas about a man in his position,' said her mother.

'Now who said I had ideas?' laughed Lee.

'You are talking about him as if you think he's marvellous.'

'Am I? Well, you can think someone marvellous without kidding yourself that they'd look at you,' she said. She looked at her watch. 'I'd best be getting back or else I shan't be considered marvellous.'

'Ta ta, everyone,' she cried, waving gaily, and set the car in motion to get her started on her return journey to her second home, for she regarded the mansion where she stayed almost as such.

Lee arrived back and was beginning to take all the shopping from her car when she was aware that there was someone behind her and turning quickly saw that it was Brad. He looked less grim-faced after a sleep. He had changed into causal clothes — well cut though casual. He had just shaved and looked even more handsome than she had imagined.

'Just a sec, Lee,' he said. 'You don't mind my calling you Lee?'

'Of course not,' she said.

'I wondered if you would spare me a few minutes?'

'Yes,' she said, looking surprised. What could he have to talk to her about on such a short acquaintance? She remembered what Phillip had said and wondered if he was going to start using his charms immediately.

'Just pop those parcels back in the car and come for a walk with me,' he said in a tone that brooked no argument.

Lee did as he had suggested and found herself being taken by the arm and led across the lawns towards the small stream which ran through the bottom of the garden. There was a rustic bridge across the stream which led them on to open countryside.

'I want to get away from the house to talk to you,' he said, and Lee thought they were surely far enough away now. There would be no eavesdroppers round here. What could he have to say to her that needed such secrecy?

On the path was a delapidated old park seat and he drew her down to sit on it after making sure that it was not too dirty to soil her clothes.

'Whose idea was it to send that letter to me advising me that my mother had had a blackout?' he asked.

'Mine,' she said, and imagined that he looked a little disappointed.

'I thought perhaps my mother or Phillip had asked you to let me know.'

'Your mother is not aware that I wrote to you, but I mentioned to Phillip that you ought to know and then you could please yourself whether you came, but I didn't think it fair not to let you know.'

'And Phillip gave you my address? It

was good of you to be so thoughtful,' he said. 'What do you think caused my mother to black out?'

'I couldn't say,' said Lee. 'The doctor isn't treating the matter as very serious. He admits that he can't find anything seriously wrong with your mother. Her heart is okay and they took blood tests which proved all right.'

'Is she worrying over anything?'

Lee was thoughtful for a moment. 'Maybe she is worrying over financial problems. The estate is being subsidised because overheads are more than income at the moment.' She hesitated and looked troubled.

'What is it?' he asked.

'Should I be discussing family affairs with you like this?'

'Of course, I'm family aren't I?'

'I know but . . .'

'Oh, I've no doubt you've heard some fine stories about me,' he said, 'but for all that I am concerned about my family. And because I left home I was not cut off without the proverbial shilling, you know. My father has left everything to my mother and nothing comes to Phillip or myself while she's alive except for an equal amount of money he left to both of us. Mother is not old and should live for years if she's not worried over anything. I do not depend upon the estate in any way, you understand? But I should hate to see it run down. There's no reason why things should be in a bad way.'

'There's a recession in this country and everyone is having difficulties,' said Lee.

'I'm aware of that, but there should be no problems in the running of the estate. High interest rates have hit industrialists who rely on loans to run their business, but there were no debts here when I left. My father and I quarrelled about the running of the estate and he was absolutely furious with me because I invested in thousands of pounds worth of modern equipment to run the place. It was a good investment and I planned to hire out the equipment to nearby farmers who couldn't afford to buy their own. That should be a good source of income. Do you know if that has been done? Has any equipment been out on hire?'

'Not that I am aware of but I haven't made it my business to go into things. I keep the accounts up to date for Phillip, but I don't know anything about the running of the estate in detail.'

'Phillip is like my father,' said Brad. 'My father didn't move with the times. He wanted to be a gentleman farmer but competition is so fierce these days every ounce of effort needs to be put into a concern to make it a success. Hiring out equipment could have been a good thing, a business on its own. I tried to argue my father into changing his methods but it was no use. We had bitter arguments. You were here when he died?'

'Yes.'

'And no doubt you thought it terrible

that I didn't come home for the funeral. As it happened I was ill with a fever and couldn't come and I thought it best not to when I was better because it might have upset my mother to see me, knowing that my father and I had been at loggerheads. I'm thankful that I wasn't here when he died for I'm sure I'd have been blamed for his death. He was a stubborn man but I cared about him a lot. And I've worried about the estate for I knew it needed someone with a go-ahead attitude and firmness to keep it going.'

Lee could imagine that. Phillip was very autocratic in his ways. Perhaps he got the best out of the men who worked on the estate, but she didn't know anything about that side of the business.

'Your mother is glad to see you now, Brad, in spite of what might have happened in the past. I can see that.'

'Do you think so?' he asked, his eyes lighting up a little.

'Yes. She told me that your father

missed you as much as she did when you left.'

His eyes misted a little and he said, 'Thanks for telling me. There wasn't so much bitterness as I thought then?'

Lee hesitated. As far as his mother was concerned she didn't feel that there was any bitterness now, but she couldn't say that as far as Phillip was concerned. 'Your brother,' she said, 'seems to have a grudge against you,' and she smiled to make it sound not too bad that he should have.

'If I tried to put Phillip on the right track he would quarrel with me as fiercely as my father did. I've been over the fields which should be turned over and ready for the crops to go in by now so that the farm equipment can be put out on loan to those who cannot afford such expensive equipment.'

'That's between you and your brother,' said Lee. 'I don't think I ought to be involved in the discussions concerning the running of the estate.'

'But you could influence Phillip,

surely. He would listen to you whereas he would accuse me of being high-handed and poking my nose in where it isn't wanted.'

'If you have the right to advise on the running of the estate you should assert your authority where you think there could be improvements.'

'Oh, there could be improvements,' he said, without hesitation. He rose, letting her see that he was ready to return to the house. 'I wondered if Phillip had put you up to writing to me in order to get me over here to help him out; he certainly needs to get cracking if he hopes to have a successful year this year. I can't think what he's playing at. The weather's grand for farmers to get their land ready.'

As they approached the house Phillip came towards them with a face like a thunder cloud. 'Where have you been?' he asked, addressing Lee and looking at her as if she'd committed a crime.

'We've been getting to know each

other,' said Brad, calmly. 'I've been saying that it's time the fields were ready for planting the crops. You won't get better weather conditions than you have at the moment.'

'I'm waiting for Daniel. He's been a bit run-down this year.'

'You can't afford to wait,' said Brad. 'Why don't you plough the fields?'

'Me?' cried Phillip. 'I've never done that sort of work.'

'You should,' said Brad. 'It's a job I enjoy and it saves paying for labour if you can do it yourself. Labour charges are high these days; it's high wages that are crippling those who have to pay them.'

'How can I do everything?' asked Phillip, sullenly.

'Well, what's been holding you up? What's stopping you today from having a go?'

'You forget that there are all the administrative jobs to attend to and the keeping of the accounts.'

'Lee does the accounts,' said Brad.

Phillip looked at Lee accusingly and she coloured.

'Oh, Lee didn't tell me that,' said Brad. 'Mother did. I've been going through the ledgers with her. Very well kept they are, too. You have some problems though.'

'Everyone has problems these days.'

'Some do through no fault of their own. But if you have problems the fault lies with you, Phillip.'

'How do you make that out?'

'We can't discuss that at the present time. But if you want to get this place going as a profitably run estate I can advise you. I have been working as a business consultant for some time.'

'I guessed if you arrived on the scene you would start disorganising everything.'

'Not disorganising, Phillip, reorganising. Believe me I wouldn't interfere if only you were concerned, but mother is worried over the way things are going and maybe that was the cause of her having that blackout. Such things can be caused by stress and strain.'

'The stress and strain has fallen on me, not mother.'

'You're wrong, Phillip. Mother is no fool. She knows things are going downhill fast. If you don't take advice from me or someone else there will be nothing for you to run here. You'll have to sell out and you know how that would affect mother.'

'Well, we'll discuss things with mother later,' said Phillip, looking at Lee pointedly.

Realising that it was embarrassing having an outsider present when they were discussing such confidential matters Lee told them she would walk on in front and get the shopping from her car.

But Phillip reached the car at the same time as she did and turned her round. 'What were you doing with Brad talking out there?' he asked, looking furious.

'He invited me to go for a walk with him to talk about things in general,' she

42

said, noticing that Brad had walked on and into the house.

'I told you to watch him.'

'I couldn't be rude to your brother and tell him I didn't want to speak to him, Phillip,' she protested, objecting to the way he was holding on to her arm. 'It would have looked most strange. What could I have said? Phillip doesn't wish me to speak with you?'

'You could have made some excuse. He's come here to make mischief.'

'I don't think so, Phillip,' she said. 'He seemed genuinely concerned about the losses being made and anxious to help.'

'He was always giving advice where it wasn't wanted.'

'You think his advice is not worth anything?'

'We don't want him,' said Phillip, firmly. 'My mother told him to go and leave us in peace two years ago and we've had peace while he's been away but now he's back all our troubles will start again.'

'I think you shouldn't be too hasty to dismiss his advice, Phillip. If he could stop losses being incurred it would be far more satisfactory than running things at a loss.'

'If anything could have been done to improve matters don't you think I would have done something before now?' he demanded with a ferocious look on his face. It was obvious he objected to Lee daring to think that Brad's advice should be considered in any way.

Lee sighed. 'It's nothing at all to do with me, Phillip. I think you should argue things out with Brad.'

'Yes. That's what it's going to be now he's back. Nothing but arguments as it was before.'

'Will you help me carry these parcels, Phillip?' she asked, hoping to get him off the subject.

He took the parcels from her and she followed, heavily laden, too, and as they went in together she saw Brad standing watching them with a speculative look on his face. He was probably wondering what they'd been talking about the same as Phillip had wanted to know what she and Brad had been talking about.

Having deposited all the shopping in the kitchen and leaving it for Mrs Palmerston's approval Lee went off upstairs. In her room she removed the high-heeled shoes she had been wearing to replace them with some comfortable house slippers and then she sat thinking about Phillip and Brad. It was a pity they couldn't agree. She hadn't taken very much notice of the way things were going on the estate for it was only her job to enter everything into the ledgers but she was more aware of the problems now that Brad had pointed them out, or some of them. She had known that they were working on capital instead of income from the different farms which brought in rents, and the profits which should have been coming from the Palmerston farm, but it hadn't really dawned on her that that state of affairs couldn't continue. No one would continue working at a loss if they had any sense, yet Phillip had seemed not to bother unduly about having to dig into their private capital month after month to keep their heads above water.

Perhaps that was why his mother had had that blackout. Brad had soon come to the conclusion that it was probably worry and strain that had caused it, yet Phillip had seemed insensitive to the fact that his mother was concerned over financial problems. Lee herself had not considered them serious because Phillip had never seemed unduly worried, but now she realised that it was a very alarming state of affairs which should have made Phillip worried.

All the months she had been working here there had never been any mention of crisis from Phillip, yet in one day Brad had taken a look at the ledgers and had pointed out to her that something needed to be done at once.

At dinner there was no mention of financial problems and Lee supposed that Phillip had requested Brad to refrain from talking on such subjects in her presence. She didn't mind that for it was only natural that family problems were the concern of the family only. There was little conversation during the meal. Mrs Palmerston told Lee she was happy with all that she had purchased from town and mentioned that she had to go to a meeting tomorrow afternoon and would like Lee to accompany her.

She often took Lee with her to various meetings to take notes and keep accounts of various organisations of which her employer was the treasurer. Lee couldn't help wondering if these organisations would be so keen to allow Mrs Palmerston to attend to their financial affairs if they had known that her own private affairs were in such a state.

After dinner, Brad announced that he was going out. Later Lee saw him looking very distinguished in his evening suit and could imagine that he would turn many a female head that evening. Phillip was in earnest conversation with his mother so Lee went upstairs to her room for a quiet read.

She turned over the pages of the book but discovered that she had no idea what she was supposed to be reading about. It seemed that the peace and quiet had been disturbed with Brad's appearance and yet she couldn't think it was such a bad thing. He wouldn't be complacent and let things go from bad to worse, she didn't suppose. But then again perhaps he had no intention of staying all that long. She wondered why her thoughts kept turning to Brad, and why she was seeing him in her mind's eye looking smart and drawing all the girls towards him because of his magnetic personality. She tried to concentrate on her book but her mind was too active to lose itself in a world of fantasy.

Phillip had stated that he would take her out more but he hadn't mentioned anything about taking her out this evening and she was glad about that. She had never seen Phillip look so outstandingly handsome, even in an evening suit, as his brother had looked tonight. The thought of being escorted by a man like Brad was more exciting than the thought of going out with Phillip.

Phillip had been right to warn her about falling for Brad's charms, she supposed, for already he was occupying her thoughts too much, and she knew that the competition amongst females for his attentions would be too great for the likes of her to get a look in. She imagined him tonight surrounded by gorgeous girls all trying to gain his attention. It would be wonderful to be the one he chose to spend his life with. And then she laughed at her own thoughts, because she was wishing she could be the one and the thought of belonging to such a gorgeous male herself was simply ludicrous. She had no possible chance, but it was nice to dream. He would pick up some raving beauty, she had no doubt, and she wondered why he hadn't already done that. But perhaps he had. How did she know that he wasn't married? But if he was, Phillip wouldn't have considered it necessary to warn her that he would try to win her affection from himself. As if she would be so lucky!

She thought about the girl he had stolen from Phillip. Had he treated her abominably? It would be so easy for a girl to transfer her love from Phillip to Brad and then to be let down must be absolutely devastating. She would heed Phillip's warning, she decided.

Lee felt decidedly restless and she rarely felt like that. Usually she found plenty of jobs to do, or jobs were found for her, and if she had an hour to spare she loved reading, but she didn't think that even her favourite authors could have held her attention this evening.

When she went downstairs later she heard Phillip and his mother still engaged in conversation.

'He actually told me to go out and work on the fields like a common labourer,' said Phillip, grumbling like a little child who has been given a disagreeable job to do. 'I wouldn't know the first thing about driving a tractor.'

If he had been her brother, Lee would have retorted, 'Well, now's your time to learn,' but she supposed it would be beneath the dignity of the son of the owner of the Palmerston estate to be seen doing menial work.

When Mrs Palmerston saw Lee she invited her to come and sit with them and Lee noticed that she looked tired and strained. She hadn't seen her look so strained before, not even before or after she'd had that blackout and Lee wondered if it had been a terrible strain seeing her eldest son again and if she was worried that once more he would start quarrels and arguments, upsetting the peace of the home.

Her employer switched on the television and they listened to the news. Nothing more was said about Brad and what he'd been suggesting and Phillip engaged Lee in conversation, which was quite a change. Usually he was out at night and if he took her she always felt it was at his mother's instigation and couldn't help feeling it was a duty he performed. He would be polite to her and nothing more, but suddenly he was beginning to converse with her as if he was really interested in her opinions and was interested in her as a person instead of just an employee of the family. Lee wasn't sure that she liked this change of relationship. She had been perfectly happy the way things had been before. She was one of the few girls who didn't have a crush on her boss.

Either Phillip or his mother had told Brad that Lee was almost one of the family and Phillip was certainly making it appear so this evening. She found herself examining him more closely as he talked to her, comparing his features with those of his brother and she decided that Phillip took after his father and Brad after his mother though Mrs Palmerston wasn't all that distinguished looking to have produced such a marvellous looking son.

Phillip's light brown hair, almost sandy looking, wasn't thick like his brother's and his eye lashes were very fair so that his eyes didn't have such a strong effect on her as those of his brother. Brad's lashes were thick and dark making his deep blue eyes look even darker. Phillip had quite a lot of freckles, which she hadn't noticed before because she hadn't studied him so intently, and there were freckles on the backs of his hands, too.

She was so absorbed in taking in his features and comparing them with his brother's that she lost the gist of what he was saying and when he waited for an answer to his question she flushed and had to admit that she hadn't caught the question.

'I'm sorry,' she said. 'I'm tired, Phillip, you must excuse me.'

'It's all right,' he said, shortly. 'I know you weren't very interested in what I was saying. Your thoughts were miles away. I suppose you were thinking about Brad and what he was talking about when you went for that walk with him.'

'I wasn't honestly,' she insisted, feeling just a little sorry for Phillip then, because she had been thinking of Brad and there must have been many girls in the past whose attention was diverted from Phillip to his handsome brother.

'I really am tired because I did a lot of shopping this afternoon and then I rushed round to see my parents,' she said.

'Yes, we take advantage of you, Lee,' said his mother. 'I realised I'd given you an extra long list to attend to today. I don't know what we'd do without you. I do hate shopping and it's marvellous to have someone to do it for me.'

'I enjoy my job,' said Lee. 'It's far

more interesting than doing a routine office job day after day. I daresay there are lots of girls who would give anything to change places with me.'

'I've been telling her that I intend to take her out and see that she has more pleasure,' said Phillip.

'Yes, I think you should, Phillip,' said his mother, giving Lee a smile. 'And now I think you'll have to excuse me because I'm tired, too. I'll take my drink up with me.'

That left Phillip and Lee to have their supper alone together and she couldn't remember ever having had supper alone with him before. Mrs Robinson came in with the trolley and they were sitting there cosily eating a light snack when Brad returned.

'You're back early, aren't you?' said Phillip, looking quite displeased to have this cosy little tête à tête with Lee broken up. 'I didn't think you'd be back for hours yet.'

'It's nearly midnight,' declared Brad, 'and I intend to be up early in the morning, if you don't.'

'Shall I pour you some coffee?' asked Lee.

'No, thanks, I've had what I want. I won't disturb you two.'

Lee felt annoyed. She didn't want him to think there was anything between herself and his brother.

He wished them goodnight and went off to bed and Lee said it was time they went, too. Phillip didn't invite her to stay a little longer talking to him. He seemed very satisfied with himself and she had the feeling that he had arranged for Brad to find them together like this seeming to be having a very intimate conversation. He wanted to give Brad the impression that there was something serious between himself and their employee and she felt very annoyed about it, yet why it should annoy her she couldn't imagine because it really didn't matter what Brad thought.

3

Lee was up early the next morning in order not to miss her usual canter over the fields. She hoped Phillip would give it a miss this morning, which he often did, but he was there waiting for her. She found this extra attention he was giving her rather annoying. She had felt free and easy in the Palmerston household but that feeling would go if she felt she was being pursued by Phillip. Now Brad, she thought, with a mischievous smile playing round her mouth, well, he would be different. It would be rather fun if he started pursuing her.

There was a slight suggestion of mist in the air to give promise of a warm sunny day although it was still very early in the year. Phillip pointed out that very often when the nice weather started too soon it petered out and they had no real good summer, but Lee was determined to take each day as it came and to get the most out of it.

As they set off on their chosen horses there was the sound of a tractor at work not far away. Phillip turned to her with a look of surprise. 'Sounds as if Daniel has changed his mind and decided to get cracking after all,' he said. 'I'm glad of that. We're very much behind with the work this year.'

As they neared the field they saw that almost half of the huge area had been ploughed. 'Goodness,' said Phillip, 'he must have started almost before it was light.'

It was surprising because Daniel, she knew, wasn't a reliable worker and pleased himself a great deal. He wasn't employed full-time by Phillip, only on a freelance basis and very often was working for someone else when Phillip needed him.

Phillip guided his horse towards the ploughed field and they waited for the tractor to come up from the other end. As it approached, Lee's keen eyes saw before Phillip's that it was not Daniel driving the tractor. As it got nearer she knew her eyesight had not played her false, it was Brad coming towards them. His hair was awry, he was wearing an old sweater and he waved cheerily as he saw them waiting there.

Looking at Phillip, Lee saw that his face was set in anger. He was furious. Why should he resent Brad getting on with an essential job? It was good of him to bother when he was only home on a short visit to see his mother. This was his holiday.

'Good afternoon,' called Brad, smirking cheekily, and letting them know he'd been up for hours.

'Daniel's not going to like this,' said Phillip. 'He'll probably not work for me again.'

'Serves him right,' said Brad. 'You won't miss him. I went to see him last night and he had all sorts of excuses for not starting on the fields so I told him not to bother, I'd do it myself. It will save you a lot.'

'You're being very high-handed, Brad,' said Phillip.

'You think so? I talked with mother and she agreed that there was no time to waste. You should have a go yourself, Phillip. It's quite a satisfying job.'

Without another word Phillip turned his horse away and moved off. Lee caught Brad's smile and returned it, and then with a shrug, turned and followed his brother.

'Blasted cheek!' cried Phillip, when they were a distance away from Brad who had started back down the field again.

'Has he no claim on the estate then?' asked Lee, knowing full well that Brad had informed her that his father had wanted the estate to go to both of them when anything happened to Mrs Palmerston.

Phillip looked at her sharply. 'What do you mean?'

'Oh, I don't mean to pry,' she said, quickly. 'I just wondered if the estate belonged to you and your mother and that Brad had no part in it.'

'Everything was left to mother,' said Phillip.

He had evaded the question for she knew that Brad had not been cut off without the proverbial shilling as he had termed it. Brad had just as much right to take control as Phillip. More if he had talked the matter over with his mother before commencing to plough the field. Perhaps Brad was making sure there was something left to take control of in the years to come.

Phillip was moody and ill-tempered and Lee wished she were on her own. She enjoyed these early morning rides which gave her an appetite for breakfast and made her feel good for the day, but Phillip put a damper over everything for her with his sulky expression.

When they got back to the house and the smell of bacon and eggs greeted them Lee turned to Phillip. 'I wonder if

Brad will be coming in for breakfast.'

Phillip looked at her and said, sarcastically, 'Thinking of taking some down to him and a flask of tea?'

'I would do that if he wanted me to,' she retorted. 'He might consider it too much trouble to come all the way back to the house if he's anxious to get the field finished.'

His mother appeared and Phillip snapped, 'Did you know that Brad intended to plough the fields himself?'

'He did mention it,' she said, in a placating tone, not wishing to upset Phillip.

'What happens when he's not here? I'll be lucky to get Daniel to come and work for me again.'

'Well, he's not a reliable worker, Phillip,' said his mother, 'and Brad knows, as well as we all do, that you have to take advantage of good weather in this country and get the crops in as soon as you can. We could have weeks of rain after this nice spell, I don't have to tell you that, and you know what that means. Neither Daniel nor anyone else would be able to plough fields that are saturated.'

'I don't think it's good for our image to be doing this sort of job ourselves,' said Phillip.

'Your father would have agreed, Phillip. He believed in having authority over the workers and letting them see who was boss, but everything is changing. Wages are too high to be able to pay for labour as we used to. If we are to survive we have to cut down on expenditure and increase our income. Brad says that can be done by taking on some of the work ourselves.'

'I can see he's been filling your head with his ideas.'

'I listened to Brad yesterday instead of flaring into a temper as your father used to every time he was crossed, and Brad talks common sense. He could see that our livestock was not good enough and that we were not utilising the land to the best advantage. Brad tells me that amongst other things he works as a consultant and he goes into the details of all sorts of businesses and advises people on ways to get better results from the resources available. People pay him for his advice which we threw back in his face.'

'He can keep it, as far as I'm concerned.'

'Phillip, I have to listen to Brad. Things have been going from bad to worse for a long time. Your father wasn't making profits and lots of the capital that has gone into this estate was mine. I didn't mind helping out now and then. I felt it was my duty to do so, but the way things are going these days I shall have nothing in a few years time.'

'We know that part of the land is likely to be released from the green belt restrictions and you'll make a fortune when you can sell the land for building purposes.'

'Your father talked for years of selling off some of the land to property developers. Maybe the time will come when it will be possible to sell at a high price, but until that time comes we have to survive, and as Brad pointed out many times, once the land is sold you've had it. You can't use that land to make any more money.'

'It would help to run the land still belonging to us.'

'We shouldn't have to pay out all the time. The land should be yielding a profit for us.'

'Are you going to let Brad take charge?'

'Brad has his own interests. But for once I listened to him. Previously I only knew that life was unbearable with constant rows and arguments. I never knew why he and his father didn't agree but I knew that your father was excitable, that he had high blood pressure, and I was afraid that Brad might push him too far and that he'd have a stroke. Naturally I put my husband first and felt it was best that Brad should go as he didn't agree with anyone. The arguments stopped and we had peace in one way, but I hated to think I'd sent my son away and I have often wondered if things might have been different if he'd been here for the past twelve months when things have been going from bad to worse giving me sleepless nights, Phillip, if they haven't disturbed yours.'

Phillip went out of the room with a face like thunder. His mother looked at Lee and shrugged. 'If you please one son you upset the other,' she said.

Lee went up to change and when she came back to breakfast she saw that Phillip had not yet come down for his breakfast and she wondered if he were sulking. It was awkward for Mrs Palmerston trying to please both sons.

'Brad must have started very early this morning,' said Lee. 'He had ploughed very nearly half of that west field when we got down there.'

'He was always a worker, I'll say that,' said his mother, 'and he loved harvest time. He couldn't bear to be lazy. It didn't take him long to size up the situation here and I believe he has already made arrangements to hire out some of our equipment to smaller farmers who can't afford to purchase such expensive machines. If he could stay a little while he'd soon get things sorted out. I can see now that he had no patience with his father or Phillip's methods of working.'

'What will happen when he has to leave again? I had no idea things were so bad. I feel I should take a cut in salary.'

Mrs Palmerston laughed. 'Goodness, Lee! I hope we aren't making you think we're poverty-stricken. We're not by a long chalk, but it would be ridiculous not to take notice of the writing on the wall. We have to stop losing money as we have been doing.'

Phillip eventually came in to breakfast but there was no sign of Brad and Lee felt compelled to mention it. 'Do you think someone should take him a drink or something?' she asked.

'You seem very concerned about

him,' said Phillip, nastily. 'It's his own fault if he doesn't come in for something to eat.'

'If I know Brad he took something with him,' said his mother. 'But you can take him a flask of coffee, Lee, if you like.'

'There's no need for Lee to go, I will,' said Phillip. 'I'd like to have a talk to Brad.'

'If you do I want no quarrelling,' said his mother, firmly. 'I'd rather send Lee than have you go down there causing trouble, Phillip.'

'Oh, so it's me who causes the trouble now, is it?' he snapped.

Lee could see that Phillip was really put out and she supposed it was only natural that he should feel hurt that Brad had taken charge immediately he had returned and this time his mother was backing her eldest son.

Mrs Palmerston found Lee plenty to do that morning looking up all sorts of information for the meeting they were going to that afternoon, but Lee found her thoughts wandering. She wished she could have taken the flask down to Brad and she would have liked to watch him at work for a while. Poor old Phillip was having his nose put out of joint. Lee had never considered his position before but now she supposed as a young man it wouldn't have hurt him to put his shoulder to the wheel and get on with some of the heavier work to be done instead of letting everyone see that he was the boss and above working on the land other than as a supervisor.

When she and Mrs Palmerston returned from the meeting that afternoon Brad was back in the house taking his ease, sprawled out on the huge settee. 'Are you tired?' asked his mother.

'Tired, but satisfied,' he smirked. 'I wish the nights would stay light a little longer. I want to finish that second field but it will mean having to use the light on the tractor to see what I'm doing.'

'I should think you've done enough for one day,' said his mother.

'Let's get the ploughing done,' he said, impatiently, 'and then the equipment will be available to hire out and bring in some extra cash for you.'

Considering that Brad was a big fellow and had been working out of doors all day he did not eat a terrific meal that evening. Dinner had been put forward a little as Brad wanted to go out and finish his work and Phillip was not at all pleased to have everything rearranged to suit his brother. He had been out all day and returned looking important, as if he'd been on some special mission but no one knew what it was.

'I'd like to come and see you working the tractor by artificial light,' said Lee to Brad.

'There's nothing to stop you coming along,' he told her.

'I'm taking you to the Willoughbys'

tonight,' said Phillip.

Lee looked at him in surprise. 'Oh, you didn't mention it.'

'I'm sure I did,' he said, giving her a savage look, and she supposed that was to remind her that he had said he would take her out more.

She looked at Brad and he said, 'If you want to come and watch me plough first I won't be all that long finishing off and I'll take you over to the Willoughbys. I'd like to see them, Phillip.'

Lee could see that Phillip was angry but he hadn't mentioned that he would like to take her out, and she didn't think he should take it for granted that she would fall in with his wishes at the last minute, so she said, 'That will be all right, Phillip, won't it? I'll come along with Brad later.'

He glared at her and if looks could have killed she would have dropped dead there and then.

'Wrap yourself up warm,' said Brad, as they set off. 'It will be chilly up on the tractor tonight.'

'You're not taking her up on the tractor with you?' cried Phillip.

'Why not? She wants to see a field ploughed in the dark and that's the best way to show her.'

Lee wrapped a head square round her head and had to walk sharply in order to keep up with Brad who didn't seem to realise that her legs were shorter than his. Lee never fancied the open fields when it was dark and always felt that trees looked beautiful in the day time but sinister at night and threatening with their branches reaching out in the darkness, but she didn't mind the dark at all walking along with Brad.

The tractor had been left half way across the field and she could see how far he had progressed in the work. 'If I can finish this tonight I'll be glad,' he said, 'and I must say that having company is going to make it pleasanter for me, Lee. After working so many hours it really begins to feel like hard work at the finish.'

She could understand that. Hour after hour he had gone backwards and forwards across these fields. He must have tremendous patience and she couldn't imagine Phillip doing it. Brad gave her a lift up on to the tractor. It was completely dark, but he switched on the spot light and a brilliant light shone along the field so that he could see what he was doing. He started the tractor and they moved along slowly.

'I don't want to cause trouble between you and Phillip,' he said, 'but I couldn't resist the temptation of bringing you with me for company tonight.'

'I don't feel that I'm letting him down,' she said. 'He hadn't mentioned anything about taking me to the Willoughbys, otherwise I wouldn't have asked to come and see you ploughing like this.'

Patiently Brad drove up the field and down again. 'I love this land,' he said.

'I'm glad to be home if only for a short time.'

'It must have been hard for you to leave then,' she said.

'It was, but I knew my mother was right. Father and I would never have hit it off and it was making her unhappy seeing that we didn't get on.'

'Do you like living in Brazil?'

'I made myself contented there. I'm the sort of fellow who can settle down so long as I can find something of interest to do. Phillip and I are entirely different from each other, you know. He was always the little gentleman and I was a scruff, always having to do something, and getting into mischief,' he added.

Lee watched the beam of light as they moved relentlessly on row after row and it had an almost hypnotic effect on her watching the land seeming to come towards them as they travelled by the aid of the spot light. She couldn't believe that Brad had only come home yesterday and here she was sitting beside him talking to him as if she'd known him years, and at the rate he was working all the fields would be ready for planting the crops in record time.

He wasn't going to be popular with Phillip and there was bound to be a certain amount of talk in the district. Daniel would let it be known that Brad Palmerston had ploughed the fields himself and no doubt his past life would be raked up again and gone over. There was always a lot of gossip in the country.

Of course, Brad could be doing all this to show Phillip up, make him look inferior in his mother's eyes. But Lee found it difficult to believe that. He seemed to be enjoying himself. He had weighed things up as soon as he'd studied the books and walked over the land and couldn't wait to get things moving in the right direction. He knew that the land was not being used to its best advantage. Lee hadn't realised because she had never lived on an estate like this before, but after listening to Brad she could well imagine that good managers who used their land to full capacity and took all the opportunities they could to make the land productive stood a chance of being successful. It took initiative and good hard work.

She couldn't help thinking that Phillip had been sitting back looking forward to the day when some of the land could be sold after being released from green belt restrictions. He believed they could ask a terrifically high price from the building developers but she felt that Brad would have liked to hang on to the land. The land he loved.

It was almost nine-thirty when Brad finished the last row and he turned to her, putting his arm around her waist. 'I'm glad that's done,' he said. 'I don't think I could do another row. Thanks for keeping me company tonight; it made it a pleasure instead of a chore. I have to admit I was tired and not looking forward to working most of this evening after a long day. But tonight has gone quickly, thanks to you.'

'You must have been lonely working hours and hours out here on your own.'

'I don't mind solitude, not in the daytime, anyway.'

'Do you think it's too late to go to the Willoughbys'?'

'Gosh, I forgot all about them. We'd better go. Come, we'll hurry and I'll get you there in less than half an hour. They aren't people who retire early for the night so you'll be able to have some time with them. Do you like them?'

'I've only been very occasionally with Phillip,' she admitted. 'I don't know your family's friends very well.'

'They used to have a very pretty daughter,' he said. 'I wonder if she's married now.'

'You mean Lucinda? Yes, I'm afraid she is.'

He laughed. 'You needn't sound sorry about it on my account. She was pretty and I liked her but that was all.'

He had liked a lot of girls according to Phillip and she wondered how many of them would find their hearts fluttering when they knew he was back home again.

They both washed and changed in record time. Lee changed into a fairly new Indian smock dress which had a quilted yoke and was in black and gold. It hadn't been a cheap model though she knew the friends of the Palmerstons were wealthy and to them it might seem cheap, but Phillip hadn't said it was a special affair or anything like that so she hoped she was dressed appropriately. Mrs Palmerston told her she looked very nice so that pleased her.

When Brad saw her he gave a little whistle. 'Very fetching,' he smiled. And then she was in the passenger seat beside him in the luxurious car which he had hired since he'd been in England. She felt she had been drawn quite close to him this evening, first on the tractor and now in this beautiful car.

'Do you like it?' he asked.

'Yes. Are you used to smart cars like this?'

'I like a large car. I've got long legs,' he told her, unnecessarily.

'I suppose it wouldn't be worth getting a new car for the time you'll be in England,' she said.

'No,' he said, and she hated the thought that he was only here on holiday. Life would seem very dull when he left to go back to Brazil.

Phillip came to them immediately they arrived and took possession of Lee as if she were his property. 'You've been ages,' he said, looking annoyed.

Brad relinquished her to Phillip's care and was soon surrounded by many people all eager to talk to him and find out what he'd been doing for the past two years.

'Making my fortune,' she heard him say, and she wondered if he had made a lot of money for himself abroad. Knowing how energetic and go ahead he was she wouldn't be surprised to know that he had.

It wasn't the thought that he could be wealthy that attracted Lee towards him. It was his strong personality, and then she realised for the first time how greatly she *was* attracted to him and had been from the moment she had first seen him. She felt she wanted to keep looking at him. It was very silly of her to let him have this effect upon her. Phillip had warned her that he would try to get her away from him as a sort of challenge and she must keep a firm control over her feelings. Not that she belonged to Phillip but because she couldn't belong to Brad.

She supposed any girl would find it easy to go overboard for Brad as she had done after having known him for just a few hours. He hadn't given her the impression that he wanted to flirt with her or draw her away from his brother so Phillip had nothing to worry about. Brad liked the more glamorous girls obviously, and that belief was strengthened when she saw him smiling into the eyes of the most gorgeous girl in the room. Lee saw that Phillip was also watching his brother and there was deep dislike in his eyes. Had Brad captured the interest of a girl that Phillip would have liked to be popular with?

'What have you been doing until now?' asked Phillip, turning to look at Lee.

'Why, nothing except finish that second field,' said Lee. 'What did you think we should be doing?'

'Knowing Brad I can think of all sorts of things,' he said.

'Well, you don't know me very well if you think I would do what I'm sure you are insinuating with a man I've only just met.'

'You know his little game, don't you? He's getting well in with Mother now that Dad's not here and before long he'll be taking complete charge over everything.'

'I think you're misjudging him, Phillip,' she said. 'He told me on the way here that he had hired a car because it wouldn't be worth buying one for the short time he would be in the country.'

Phillip's eyes brightened. 'Did he say that?'

'Yes. So you see, you have nothing to worry about.'

Phillip seemed in a much brighter mood after that and soon he left Lee to talk to a group of other people and she felt she was back to the unimportant person who worked for his family again. She couldn't think why he had ever put himself out to bring her amongst his friends like this unless it was to please his mother who often suggested that he took her out for a break.

Brad noticed quite soon that Lee was left stranded and immediately joined her and drew her into the circle of people to whom he was talking. And because Brad was taking an interest in her other people began to do so and she found that they weren't so stand-offish as she had imagined. It had been Phillip's attitude towards her that had influenced them to treat her almost as an outsider.

She found herself being invited to join the sports club for games of tennis and thought she might do that. It would keep her fit and agile.

When Phillip saw that Brad had taken charge of her he returned to her and again made it appear that she was with him and not Brad. He drew her away from the others and actually told her that she was looking very nice. 'Is that a new dress?' he asked.

'No. I've worn it before. You couldn't have noticed,' she said.

'I don't know why I didn't. You look great in it.'

He was like a dog in a manger, she thought. He wasn't interested in her at all until he thought someone else might be and then he wanted to make it look as if she was his exclusive property.

Until now she had been almost indifferent in her feelings towards Phillip, but at this moment she felt that she positively disliked him. He had deliberately drawn her away from Brad who had rescued her after Phillip had neglected her. She couldn't understand why Mrs Palmerston had favoured Phillip and not Brad because out of the two she was confident that Brad was superior in every way. Brad wouldn't leave her feeling an outsider in company as Phillip had so often done.

Lee had been at a disadvantage in the company of Phillip's friends, not wishing to take too much on herself and show her friendly disposition as she would do in the company of her own friends. Phillip had deliberately, until now, made her feel conscious that she was an outsider, made her feel that she was not acceptable to his friends when all the time they were quite willing to accept her. She had thought they were snobs, but they weren't.

Phillip's flattery now, pretending he admired the dress which she had worn when she had been out with him before without any comment from him meant nothing to her. Brad had told her as soon as he saw her in it that she looked very fetching and showed his admiration which she was sure meant more than any compliment Phillip might pay her.

She had no alternative but to travel back with Phillip. She would have much preferred to return with Brad who had brought her here and the look he gave her when she left at Phillip's side made her feel that he, too, would have enjoyed her company back home, but perhaps that was wishful thinking. A man like Brad wouldn't look twice at a girl like herself when he could have his pick from the most glamorous girls only too willing to throw themselves at his feet.

4

Brad followed them closely home from the Willoughbys'. Lee could see his headlights in the mirror and Phillip must have seen them, too, and knew that Brad would follow them indoors almost immediately, and it was that that made Lee confident that the kiss he gave her was for Brad's benefit, not for her own pleasure.

They were hardly in the house before Phillip drew her towards him and was giving her what would appear to Brad when he came upon them, a lover's kiss. Lee had been taken unawares, but she soon got over her surprise and pulled herself away from Phillip indignantly. How dare he assume that she would have no objections to being kissed like that?

'What's the matter?' he asked, with a detestable smile. 'You don't think Brad is shocked to find us in each other's arms?'

She looked quickly in Brad's direction. It didn't matter what Brad thought, she told herself, her indignation was directed towards Phillip for taking liberties. 'I'm off to bed,' she retorted, fearing she might say something extremely rude to Phillip. 'Goodnight!'

She lay in bed unable to sleep because her anger wouldn't allow her to relax. It was no use telling herself she was making mountains out of mole hills; she was simply furious. As she calmed down she had to admit that her anger was not so much because Phillip had kissed her, but because he had made quite sure that Brad had seen that kiss. It wasn't true to say it didn't matter what Brad thought, either, because it did. She didn't want Brad to believe there was anything between herself and Phillip. It could make no difference to her, of course, what Brad believed, but she knew that she hated him to be given the impression that there was an understanding between her and his brother.

Eventually she slept and although she was awake early the next morning decided to give horse-riding a miss. She felt she couldn't go riding with Phillip this morning. He didn't always accompany her on her early morning rides but when he had done he had always been proper in his behaviour, never giving her any reason to feel that he had any interest in her whatever which had suited her fine. She might have been peeved if she'd had a crush on him, but she couldn't imagine anyone having a crush on Phillip. They would have to be just as boring a person as he was himself to tolerate him.

To her surprise there was a knock on her door. 'Are you awake?' and to her annoyance she discovered it was Phillip.

'Yes,' she called, 'but I'm still in bed.'

'Don't be long. I'm waiting for you.'

'I'm not coming this morning, Phillip,' she replied. 'I don't feel like riding today.'

'Oh, come on,' he insisted. 'You're not still angry with me over last night, are you?'

'No,' she said, trying to be patient. 'I just don't feel like riding today.'

She was annoyed with herself for suggesting that she wasn't perfectly fit. She should have been straightforward and said, 'I don't want to come horse-riding with you, Phillip,' but she did work for him and his mother and had to be careful how she spoke to him.

Lee was a very fit person, rarely ever felt off colour, and she hated to have to pretend she wasn't feeling up to scratch. She turned over and tried to snatch an extra hour's sleep, but it was no use, and she decided she might as well get up as lie there wide awake.

She went down to the study and began to type out the minutes of the meeting which she had attended with

Mrs Palmerston the day before for she knew that her employer wanted her to type out an article she had written for a County Magazine later on.

She supposed that Brad took after his mother for having lots of energy for she belonged to so many clubs and organisations yet still found time to write for numerous magazines and papers. There was a cheque by almost every other post for Mrs Palmerston and Lee suspected now, that she was working hard turning out as many articles as she could every week in order to earn money which was going to cover the losses made in the running of the estate. Things were beginning to look clearer to her now. Phillip was living off his mother's earnings without putting himself out at all to try to make his job a success. He was having an easy life going round as the important Phillip Palmerston when in actual fact he was a parasite. Lee wondered if Mrs Palmerston had been carrying her husband, too, over the years. She spent hours on research work for different articles and perhaps this was from necessity rather than a love of writing.

You couldn't admire a man who lived off the earnings of his mother without making some effort to repay her. The study door opened and she looked up, expecting to see Phillip, probably still annoyed with her for not going riding with him that morning, but it was Brad and he'd brought her some coffee.

'I heard you typing away quite early,' he said.

'Oh, I hope I didn't disturb you.'

'No, you didn't. I was already up. You missed your horse-riding this morning?'

She smiled. 'I was too lazy to get up.'

'Phillip went out like a bear with a sore head,' said Brad. 'I'm sorry if I barged in on you last night, Lee, but I knew that you were both aware that I was immediately behind you. I didn't sneak in on you.'

'Of course you didn't.'

'You seemed annoyed.'

'I was. But not with you.'

He laughed. 'You were not in the mood for kisses, was that it?'

She nearly told him that she objected to anyone taking it for granted that she could be kissed without warning and against her will but she couldn't let him see how much she disliked his brother, it wouldn't have been nice.

Brad stayed and had some coffee with her and after a time they were joined by Mrs Palmerston who said she'd heard their voices as she came downstairs. 'No horse-riding this morning, Lee?' she asked.

'No, I wasn't in the mood,' said Lee.

Mrs Palmerston sat herself down and they discussed the weather and Brad spoke of the possibility of getting the potato crop planted during the next day or so. They planted on a rotation system and Brad began checking with his mother which fields had yielded which crops the previous year. He was amazed to learn that not all the fields had been prepared to grow anything last year.

'What a bloomin' waste,' he declared.

In the midst of this conversation Phillip walked in, still in his riding clothes. 'H'm, I can see why you didn't want to come with me this morning,' he said, grimly to Lee. 'You didn't want to miss this cosy little discussion taking place behind my back.'

'Phillip!' cried Mrs Palmerston. 'That's enough. You have a nasty suspicious mind if you think we would agree to have private discussions that do not involve you.'

'There has been plenty of talk behind my back,' he retorted, 'and plans being made without my knowing anything about them.'

'Perhaps, but not planned talks aimed to exclude you. Brad did tell me he was going to get those fields ploughed yesterday without delay and I agreed that it was necessary and this morning, just as a matter of course, we have been discussing getting the crops planted.'

'I can't see the point in flogging ourselves to death trying to make the land yield profits when there's a strong possibility of the green belt restrictions being lifted in the near future,' said Phillip.

'I wouldn't say this is the best time to sell land,' said Brad. 'From what I gathered when I was out the other night there is not only a recession in industry but in everything. House agents are finding it very difficult to sell houses so what's the point in putting up even more that they won't be able to sell? And you won't get the best price for the land while there's a slump.'

'I've been talking to a builder who would give anything for some land in this area and councillor George Thomas has promised to push ahead with getting building restrictions lifted.'

'You haven't resorted to bribery, I hope,' said Brad.

Phillip flushed dull red. 'There's no

harm in doing a man a favour if he does you one.'

'If you attempt to bribe someone in authority such as a councillor, Phillip, you are laying yourself open to a bribery and corruption charge.'

'Who's to know anything about a favour done between friends?'

'Favours such as that can be revealed years afterwards,' said Brad. 'You lay yourself open to blackmail and it isn't worth the candle. Besides, you know that the people in the village have been fighting tooth and nail to stop developers getting their hands on this beauty spot. Don't you care about them?'

'Do you think they'd care about us if they had the opportunity to cash in on anything?'

'That's not the point.' He turned to Lee. 'What do you think about selling up our land?'

'It's nothing to do with me,' she protested.

'I'm told you are almost one of the

family,' he said, looking at Phillip, so it must have been he who gave Brad the idea that she was, perhaps making Brad believe they had an understanding. 'Tell me your honest opinion, Lee,' said Brad. 'Would you or would you not sell off acres and acres of this land?'

'Not for building purposes if I could possibly help it,' she said. 'Not while there are so many acres of derelict land which could be put to use for development purposes. I think your mother would agree with me. I type out her articles and she is all for the preservation of the beauty of this country.'

'Yes, I am,' said Mrs Palmerston, 'but Phillip has been putting up a strong argument to persuade me that we need the capital more than the land.'

Phillip looked squarely at Lee. 'We need money before we can be married.'

She gasped. 'Before you and I can be married!' she cried, incredulously.

'Yes.'

'But we aren't going to be married,' she said.

'Why?' he asked. 'Why have you changed your mind?'

'I haven't changed my mind,' she snapped. 'I have never wanted or consented to marriage with you, Phillip.'

He laughed as if he couldn't believe she could say such a thing. 'And I suppose you didn't say you would need some more expensive clothes when I took you to meet my friends, and you would deny that I offered to buy you whatever you wanted?'

The colour rushed to her face. What on earth would Brad and Mrs Palmerston be thinking of her? As if she would suggest that Phillip bought clothes for her. 'I know you offered but I didn't accept your offer,' she retorted.

'Things have changed since Brad came home, haven't they?' he said.

She couldn't think what he was trying to prove. She looked at Brad who was just looking at her expressionlessly and at Mrs Palmerston who seemed puzzled. 'Will you excuse me?' she asked, and left the room hurriedly.

When she reached her room Lee found she was trembling with anger, or was it because Phillip had made her seem deceitful in the presence of Mrs Palmerston and Brad? Or was it because she hated the thought that Phillip had given the impression that Brad was the reason for her change of mind? Would Brad believe that there had been a serious talk about marriage between her and Phillip, that she had given him reason to believe that she would marry him until Brad arrived on the scene? He might think she had given Phillip that idea herself.

She sat on the bed and tried to calm herself down. What were Phillip's motives? She knew he didn't really want to marry her.

And then the truth seemed to dawn on her. Phillip had apparently been badgering his mother to sell off some of the land and that had been worrying to her. He had even gone as far as to try and influence a councillor to use his authority to get restrictions removed on the green belt area. With the arrival of Brad he would realise that his intentions would be thwarted by his older brother who was not in favour of selling their land. Phillip's excuse would be that he needed capital in order to get married and he wanted Lee to pretend that they were intending to marry.

She could think of no other reason why he should intimate that there was an understanding between them. If he wanted money to get married his mother and Brad would understand and possibly agree to the raising of capital by the sale of some of their assets, but she felt sure that as soon as Phillip had his hands on the money he would find some excuse for not going on with the wedding even if she had agreed to it, which she hadn't and never would.

Before long Mrs Palmerston came up to her room. 'Lee, breakfast is ready,' she said. 'You must be hungry; you've been up some time.'

'I don't think I could eat down there with Brad and Phillip,' said Lee. She looked up at her employer. 'Do you think I agreed to marry Phillip?' she asked.

'Not if you say you didn't,' said Mrs Palmerston, and Lee rose to thank her.

'It's nice of you to believe me for Phillip is your son, after all. Perhaps it would be better if I left. I wouldn't want to cause trouble between your sons. I swear that Brad's arrival has meant no change whatever in my attitude towards Phillip. I have never thought of him with marriage in mind and though he mentioned it to me I cannot believe that he was serious. Why you know, Mrs Palmerston, that he doesn't care for me.'

'I don't see why he shouldn't,' said his mother. 'I wouldn't object to you as a daughter-in-law, I can assure you. And I don't want you to start talking about leaving. I rely on you too much to let you go so let's hear no more nonsense about that. Come down to breakfast and just pretend nothing has been said.'

With Mrs Palmerston talking to her like that and smiling almost like a conspirator Lee found the courage to go down and have breakfast. She needn't have worried about Phillip and Brad for neither of them was at the breakfast table.

Mrs Palmerston seemed relieved, too, that they were on their own and as they ate their bacon and fried bread she began to talk about the article she had written and which she wanted Lee to type for her. 'I would like to get it off today,' she said, and then smiled. 'Funnily enough it is about conservation and the need to be less destructive in the countryside.'

'I know,' said Lee. 'People talk about the earth as if it's theirs. It amuses me when people say this is my country or my town. We really don't possess anything, do we? We are just privileged in being able to live here.'

'I'm glad to find someone who thinks as I do,' said Mrs Palmerston. 'I've never felt possessive about the land we own. I know it isn't really ours, but I love it as if it were and would like to prevent it being swallowed up by building contractors.'

'Brad said he loved the land, too,' said Lee.

Mrs Palmerston looked at her keenly and Lee found the colour rising to her face. 'That was when he was ploughing the field last night and I went with him to watch.'

'I think I misjudged Brad a great deal,' said her employer quietly. 'I listened to Phillip and his father and they made me believe Brad was a trouble-maker. And then when he moved out and took Phillip's girl with him I felt I would never forgive him. Her name was Iris and Phillip thought the world of her. She wasn't the type of girl I would have chosen for him, she overdressed and made up too much, but she was Phillip's choice and he was terribly hurt when she went away with Brad.'

'And yet Brad didn't want her,' said Lee, 'or he would have married her.'

'Yes. I can't understand that. Brad has been a bit of a lad with the girls. When he was younger he used to go off into the towns and he brought home a lot of girls he'd met there and I used to think he'd get married young. I didn't think he wouldn't bother at all.'

They went off into the study and Lee typed out the article for Mrs Palmerston and then went off to get it into the post and to do some shopping. She arrived back in time for lunch. Brad came in then but there was no sign of Phillip and Lee wondered if he had gone off in a temper or was sulking somewhere.

During lunch no one would have known there had been that outburst in the study earlier on. Brad spoke about the crops he was attending to and went on to say that he'd been talking to Bill Jones who owned a small farm near the estate. 'He told me he was waiting to hire a tractor from the Hire Plant Company but at this time of the year all the machinery was out on loan. I soon told him we had some equipment he could hire and that surprised him. He said he knew others who'd be glad to hire as well and we agreed upon a price favourable to both of us. That was the idea in the first place: to make capital out of hiring machinery out, but Phillip hasn't bothered at all and Dad couldn't have bothered, either.'

'I know your father grumbled about the expense of all that equipment.'

'If I had stayed on here I would have got that money back over and above what we paid out. Some firms make their profit simply from hiring out farm implements. And I notice lots of ours have been neglected. Left out in the open during the winter instead of being put under cover. I don't know what the men we employ are supposed to be doing. Phillip doesn't keep them up to scratch.'

'Well, you've certainly got things moving since you arrived,' said his mother. 'It's a pity Phillip resents it so much.'

'I'll be gone shortly and things will be back to what they were before.'

He looked at Lee when he said this and she supposed he believed that she had promised to marry Phillip and had changed her mind on meeting his brother but would revert back to his brother when he left. Her colour rose and she felt uncomfortable.

His mother didn't look happy at the thought of his leaving and he said, 'I'll make frequent trips back to try and get Phillip to pull his socks up, Mother.'

By the end of the day he had worked with the men and they'd got a whole field sown with potatoes, and still there was no sign of Phillip. He always talked grandly to Lee about the administrative work he did on the estate and she wondered what that entailed. Brad seemed to have worked wonders accomplishing so much in a couple of days.

Perhaps the administrative work Phillip talked about meant meeting people in authority and trying to get into their favour to get restrictions lifted on the green belt in order that agricultural land could be sold for business purposes.

Lee had missed her horse-riding and towards evening before it got dark she decided to make up for not going early in the morning and went off to the stables to saddle her favourite horse, Nelson. He was pleased to see her, nuzzling up to her and soon she was galloping away across the meadows leading to quiet country lanes.

She was glad she hadn't had to see Phillip all day since that incident in the study this morning. It was good to get away from everyone to think about it. The land was gently undulating and as she took in the beauty all around her she couldn't help wondering how Phillip could be willing to part with any of the land that belonged to them. She would have thought he would have taken great pride in it. He enjoyed riding and must surely be attached to his surroundings, or was he completely insensitive to them and for that reason could bear to sell a few acres?

It was almost dark when Lee got back to the stables. She was unsaddling Nelson, talking softly to the horse when she became aware that she was being watched. She turned and it was Phillip just standing there watching her and for a moment she felt almost fear of him. But that was stupid. He might be angry with her for not falling in with his plans but he wouldn't harm her, she felt sure.

'You let me down good and proper this morning, didn't you?' he said, nastily. 'But Brad and mother didn't believe you when you told them you hadn't agreed to marry me. Brad assured me that he would be returning to Rio soon and his plans don't include taking you with him as he took my last girl.'

'I didn't expect that they would,' she said, coldly. 'It has been you who has been insinuating that I would fall for Brad's charms, that I already have transferred my affection from you to him.'

'Don't say that you haven't,' he said, sarcastically. 'You would have jumped at the chance of marrying a man in my position if you hadn't thought Brad might be a better catch.'

'Until Brad came, Phillip, you treated me as nothing more than an employee. I can't see that there is a great difference in your attitude except that you would like your mother and Brad to think that you have proposed to me and that I accepted. I would prefer to keep our relationship as it was before. I did offer to leave this morning but your mother asked me not to so I am considering her.'

'Well, I'd like a little consideration,

too. Don't you think I could sweep a girl off her feet as Brad can?'

'I haven't thought about it,' she said. 'And Brad hasn't attempted to sweep me off my feet I can assure you.'

'You expect me to believe that?'

'It's true,' she said, turning to go, but she found herself caught up in his arms and held tightly. She tried to free herself but he was too strong for her. 'Let me go!' she cried in alarm, but he laughed and then kissed her in a brutal, insulting sort of way.

When he released her she shot at him, angrily. 'Is that supposed to be the sort of kiss to sweep a girl off her feet?'

She put her hand to her mouth which she was sure would be bruised.

'It didn't come up to expectations?' he asked. 'Well, we'll try again.'

'No, we won't,' she said, wishing she'd fled from him immediately he had released her because he caught her again and although she struggled with all her might he wouldn't let her go.

His grip was cruel and once more she was subjected to punishing kisses that were hateful.

The next time he released her she made sure he wouldn't kiss her again, and escaping him, she went running as fast as she could towards the house. She passed Brad on the way and wondered if he had witnessed those kisses. If he had they could have seemed quite passionate kisses which she welcomed from where he was and he would be thinking it strange that she should deny there was anything between herself and his brother when he had come across them kissing like that. And he had witnessed their kiss last night. How could he know that she hated his brother at that moment?

She knew that Brad stood looking after her as she raced towards the house and she was glad that Mrs Palmerston was nowhere in sight to see her distress. She fled to her room, got her car keys and went downstairs again to her car. She wanted to get away from the house. As far away as possible and never come back again.

Before she could get the car started Brad approached her. The car would act awkward and not start immediately for she wanted to drive away before he could speak to her. But he opened the car door on the passenger side and popped his head inside.

'Can anyone come with you?' he asked.

'No,' she said, in a voice choking her.

'Please,' he said, sidling into the passenger seat. 'I don't think you should be driving in the state you're in.'

So he had guessed she was upset. Without a word she started the car and shot away.

5

She drove like a maniac down the lane and Brad made no protest, showed no sign of nervousness. It was only when she reached the narrower lane which was a continuation of dangerous curves and bends that he said firmly, 'Now slow down!'

She found herself obeying his command and then, realising that her temper was cooling, she pulled the car up into an opening which led to a field and just sat there.

'What was all that about?' he asked, softly.

'I don't want to give up my job,' she said, after a pause, 'but it looks like I'll have to.'

'Why?'

She shrugged. 'Oh, your brother is making things difficult for me.'

'You mean since I came home? He's

afraid that I shall try and win you away from him?'

'He never showed the slightest sign of interest in me until you arrived,' she exclaimed.

'It didn't seem like that to me. The first time I saw you, you were returning from riding with him.'

'Yes, he's been in the habit of joining me sometimes when I've gone riding, but he's always been the boss and me the employee.'

Brad laughed. 'Perhaps you misjudge him. Phillip takes himself very seriously.'

'I never desired a different relationship and I cannot understand why Phillip has suddenly changed.'

'I should say he does think a lot of you in his way and he's afraid I'm going to steal you away as I did his last girl.'

So Brad admitted that he had done that and he wasn't ashamed of doing it. 'I'm not Phillip's girl,' retorted Lee.

'You deny there is anything between you and yet I come across you kissing here and there?' She could tell there was amusement in his voice.

'He never kissed me before you came,' she snapped.

'I take it then that Phillip forced his kisses on to you just now?' He was quite serious again. 'I knew you were upset the way you ran away from him.'

Lee didn't say anything to that. She hated to tell him unpleasant things about his own brother. 'Lee!' he said, anxiously. 'He didn't try to force you into more than kissing you?'

'No. But his kisses weren't loving ones. He was angry with me.'

'I didn't know my brother was like that,' he said, curtly.

'I don't want him to know I've been discussing it. I'd just like to leave and not have to see him again.'

'How do you think that would affect my mother? She relies on you a lot, Lee. She said you helped her get over the loss of my father.'

'That's why I'm upset,' she exclaimed.

'I like your mother. I'd do anything for her, but I can't stay if Phillip is going to behave like, well . . . be awkward.'

'I could have a word with him. Assure him that he has no need to be afraid of my presence here. I'll be gone very soon.'

She thought about that. He had been here such a short time and yet when he went she knew she for one was going to miss him very much.

'Don't you think everything will be as it was before when I've gone?' he asked, as she didn't answer him.

'Probably,' she said, 'but you can't possibly be blamed for Phillip's behaviour.'

'Oh, I can,' he said, drily. 'You'd be surprised what I've been blamed for in the past.'

'Maybe. But I think it has been a tonic for your mother, seeing you again.'

'There's only my mother that I care about,' he said.

There seemed a sadness in his voice

and she realised he must have been very unhappy being told by the one he loved the most to clear off and leave them in peace.

'Have you and Phillip never been close?' she asked.

'Not as close as most brothers are. I've tried to help him in the past, being the big brother, you know, but Phillip never wanted to accept help or advice from me. I suppose that's natural. People like to go their own way, but when there's a lot at stake it is often advisable to discuss things. He never would, though, nor my father. They turned everything into an argument.'

He sounded genuinely fond of Phillip and his father and it was hard to reconcile that with the fact that he had stolen his brother's girl.

'Do you think Phillip's interest lies elsewhere? Perhaps he is not the type to work on the land.'

'If he has any terrific ambitions to do something else he has never talked about them,' said Brad. 'It seems to me that it suits Phillip very well to be a country gentleman. He should have lived in the last century.'

'And yet he can't be as fond of the country as you are or he'd not be anxious to sell some of the land.'

'That's true enough. But he can't sell the land you know without our mother's permission, and I doubt whether she would give it to him now. She had been thinking about it and was concerned, believing that was the only way out of their present situation, but we have discussed it and I think she's changed her mind. I shall be keeping my eye on things from now on, with her permission, and we'll get the land producing a profit this year, all being well. Phillip could manage far more cattle, he has plenty of grazing land. There'll be a turning point in the running of the Palmerston estate, you'll see.'

'How can you keep an eye on things if you're in Brazil?'

'I shall come over frequently. Once

the crops are planted it's a waiting game until we reap the harvest. I could come over then. I doubt whether Phillip intended to make full use of the land this year. He's just been marking time until he could raise some money on the sale of the land which no doubt would fetch an enormous sum if building restrictions were lifted. But you agree with me and my mother that it would be a shame to let the builders start spoiling the landscape with housing estates.'

'Phillip is going to be very disappointed.'

'I'm afraid he is. But perhaps when he knows that he is not going to gain any capital the easy way he'll start doing some really hard work. You can make money breeding the right sort of animals, taking advice from experts. I'm always willing to learn everything I can for improvement. Another thing that's worrying is that Phillip hasn't bothered to see to the maintenance of farmhouses which are rented from us. It is false economy to neglect to keep property in good repair. This was another source of argument between me and my father. I arranged for some property repairs at one time and he was furious at the cost, and yet those houses would have been in such a bad state today if they hadn't been renovated that they would have to be demolished instead of which they are still standing and bringing in the rents.'

'I've often thought myself that the land isn't being utilised to full advantage,' said Lee. 'I have often been fruit picking with my friends and there have been crowds of people picking their own fruit. Some farms have their own stalls to sell their own produce, but there's nothing like that here.'

'You're a girl after my own heart,' he declared. 'You can see ways and means of making the best of things.'

It pleased her to know that he didn't regard her as a nit-wit but he couldn't fill her with the desire to go back to the house to meet Phillip again. She gave a deep sigh and he said, 'What's that for?'

'I'm just wondering what to do. I intended to get right away from the house and not go back after I'd got rid of my fury. But I shall have to go back to fetch my clothes and all my belongings.'

'You won't have any more trouble from Phillip, I promise.'

'I don't want to cause trouble between you two.'

'You won't. I shall just make it quite clear to Phillip that my stay here is only temporary and that he has no need to fear that I have my beady eyes on you.'

Lee didn't know whether she liked to hear him say that. He was supposed to have an eye for the girls but he was letting her see that he had no interest in her. Perhaps the stories of his escapades with the girls had been exaggerated the same as his other so-called bad points. Give a dog a bad name. He could be letting her know that he had more respect for her than to play with her affections.

'Come on. Turn the car round and let's go back,' he said. 'Try and put up with Phillip for my mother's sake. You don't have to stand just anything from him, but he needs you to keep those accounts in order for him.'

Brad's voice was persuasive and so Lee started the car and reversed to go back in the direction of the house again.

When she pulled up on the drive she said, 'Don't upset Phillip by letting him know all that I've been saying about him, will you?' She couldn't hurt Phillip's feelings although she didn't care for him.

'Not if that's what you wish,' said Brad, 'although I think I should tell him not to force kisses on you that you don't want.'

'Please don't mention it.'

'Very well.'

He was out of the car before her and waited for her. 'How would you like me to give you a nice kiss to wipe out those you didn't want?' he asked.

She couldn't see his face clearly in the darkness and wondered whether he was just teasing. But he had his hands on her shoulders and repeated his question. She felt the strong male attraction as he stood close to her and lifted her face to his. He took her silence as an invitation and drew her close into his arms and the kiss he gave her was far, far different from the kisses Phillip had forced upon her. She believed Brad had only intended to give her a light kiss, but felt him give a deep sigh as he released her, and then he drew her close to kiss her again, obviously as carried away as she was.

He held her close for a moment before releasing her and that closeness had a terrific effect on Lee. No one had made her feel like that before. She felt like clinging to him and asking him to kiss her again. Her face had become warm and the whole of her body seemed to glow with warmth.

'That was nice, Lee,' he murmured.

But there was no repeat performance because the door leading into the yard opened and the light spilled out upon them as Phillip came striding out. 'Where have you been?' he snapped at Lee.

'She was going for a little spin and I asked her to take me with her,' said Brad. 'You don't mind, do you?'

'I was going to take you into town for a meal, Lee, but it's too late now,' he grumbled.

'You never said,' she replied, and walked past him into the house leaving the two brothers confronting each other. Brad had promised not to mention their conversation and she felt sure he wouldn't.

In her room she stood trying to recapture the thrill of his kisses. It was no use Phillip or anyone else telling her not to succumb to his charms, she just hadn't been able to help herself. How many girls had felt like that about him? She didn't suppose a kiss like that meant anything at all to him, but it had had a devastating effect on her.

He had said he would give her a nice kiss to wipe out the kisses she didn't want and funnily enough his kisses had made her forget those cruel ruthless ones Phillip had given her and she was now beginning to wonder if she'd made mountains out of mole hills. Anyway, she was glad she hadn't gone racing back home for there were no explanations to make now and although Phillip hadn't sounded all that pleased when he saw her with Brad he had said he'd been planning to take her out for a meal.

Lee was still wearing her riding-habit and decided to have a shower and change into a neat little green woollen dress which was useful for when the evenings grew cooler. It was early in the year and was often quite cold in the evenings.

When she entered the sitting-room she realised that both Brad's and Phillip's eyes were upon her and felt her colour rise. She was not used to such attention from the opposite sex though she had had plenty of boy friends. Phillip moved towards her and said, 'You look lovely in that dress, Lee.'

'Thank you,' she said, and instead of looking into Phillip's eyes she found herself looking straight into those of his brother.

Phillip switched on a tape of the Nolan sisters and Lee sat down prepared for a musical evening. Mrs Palmerston joined them and it was a nice cosy family gathering. No one would have thought there were any undercurrents, they seemed in perfect harmony.

Phillip was being extra charming to Lee. She had never known him put himself out so much and it didn't please her. It was easy to push him away when he was being objectionable but you can't be nasty to someone putting himself out to be nice to you.

He came and sat close to her and said, softly, 'I'm sorry about the way

I behaved earlier.'

She didn't think he was, really. She couldn't imagine Phillip being sorry about anything, and yet she knew it wouldn't be easy for him to apologise to her.

'Am I forgiven?' he asked, looking quite meek, and she felt like smacking his face and yelling, 'No, you're not.'

Lee evaded the question and turned instead to answer a question Mrs Palmerston put to her.

'Do you know what I fancy?' said Brad.

'What?' asked his mother.

'Some fish and chips. I'd like to eat them out of the paper as I used to. You don't get fish and chips anywhere else as they do them in England.'

Lee looked at him and laughed. 'You've made me fancy some, too.'

'Let's go and get some, shall we, Phil? Let's all go, you as well, Mother.'

Phillip hesitated. Lee felt sure it would be beneath his dignity to eat fish and chips from the paper wrapping with his fingers, but seeing that the others were in favour he said, 'Right. Let's go then.'

They all went in Brad's hired car. Lee would have loved to sit in the front beside Brad, but she got in the back with Mrs Palmerston who was quite amused at the thought of going for a run into town with her sons for fish and chips.

When the brothers left the car to go together into the crowded fish and chip shop Mrs Palmerston said, 'You don't know how happy it makes me to see my two sons as friendly as they are tonight.'

'That is how brothers should be,' said Lee. 'We are a very happy family. We argue amongst ourselves at times, but we don't quarrel.'

'I suppose my husband and I are to blame for Phillip and Brad being so difficult. We should have been firmer when they were young.'

'They have entirely different tempera- ments,' said Lee. 'It's doubtful whether you could have prevented them from disagreeing with each other.'

'It's nice of you not to make me feel I've failed in my job as a mother,' said Mrs Palmerston, fondly.

Phillip came out of the shop and opened the car door to ask, 'Salt and vinegar?'

'Yes, please,' laughed his mother, and Lee said, 'And for me.'

Shortly afterwards a packet of fish and chips was placed in their hands and Brad told them to start eating them at once before they got cold. Lee couldn't help giggling. She had often bought and eaten fish and chips from the paper before she'd got home when she'd been with her own friends, but it seemed most strange to be sitting in this luxurious car eating them with her employer and her sons.

They were absolutely delicious and they sat eating without talking until they'd eaten every bit of fish and every single chip.

Brad collected their wrappings and

went to put them in a litter bin outside the shop. He came back rubbing his hands together and as he got into the car he laughed. 'The car stinks of fish and chips.'

When they arrived home, Mrs Palmerston went into the kitchen laughing, to make some tea. 'I like tea after fish and chips,' she said, 'instead of coffee.'

They all ended up in the kitchen. Mrs Robinson had retired for the night and they had to wait on themselves. 'I don't know when I've enjoyed myself so much,' said Mrs Palmerston.

Brad put his arm around her waist. 'Is that a highlight, going out for fish and chips?'

'Yes,' she smiled. 'I'm glad you thought of it.'

'You'll have to see that Mother has more little trips out like that, Phillip,' said Brad. 'I shall have to be getting back to Rio soon.'

His mother didn't look at all pleased about that, but Lee was sure that

Phillip was delighted.

'Can't you stay with us a little longer, Brad?' asked his mother. 'You have been away so long.'

He looked at her with eyebrows raised. 'Don't tell me you missed me. It was you who told me to go.'

'I missed you,' she said. 'I wanted you to go because of all the unpleasantness but I didn't expect you to go to the other side of the world and not see us for a couple of years.'

'Surprising how the time goes,' he said. 'Now that I'm back it doesn't seem five minutes since I went away.'

'And do you have to go back so soon?'

'I have lots of business interests out there, Mum. I can't leave them in the charge of someone else for too long. No one works as well as you do yourself.'

Lee could imagine that he liked to be in control and that he put every ounce of energy into his work as he had done here in the short time he'd been at home.

Mrs Palmerston was quiet and he said, 'I've asked you to come with me, Mother. Why don't you? And bring Lee with you.'

'And what would I do if both of them went off with you?' snapped Phillip.

'You don't begrudge mother a trip abroad do you, Phil?' Brad asked.

'But you're talking of taking Lee as well.'

'Lee would be company for Mother while I was working. You can get yourself another part-time secretary, surely. Or do the accounts yourself until she comes back.'

Phillip looked at his mother and Lee, anxiously, but she didn't say whether she would consider going or not.

'I think I'm going off to bed,' said Lee. 'It seems to have been a long day to me.'

'See you bright and early in the morning,' said Phillip. 'No missing your ride in the morning.'

Lee looked at him dubiously. She

didn't relish the idea of going horse-riding with him again. If he was objectionable she would wish she hadn't gone, but on the other hand, she didn't want him to be nice to her. She felt in an awkward situation.

'I'll join you tomorrow,' said Brad. 'I haven't ridden for ages.'

Phillip gave him a fierce look but he couldn't very well say that he didn't want him to join them. Lee was delighted. With the two of them she would feel much safer.

'See you in the morning then,' cried Lee, as she wished them all goodnight and went off to her room. It had been a pleasant evening after all. She had wondered how she was going to be civil to Phillip but it hadn't been so difficult. Brad had helped her over that embarrassment and she had a feeling he had offered to join them horse-riding so that she wouldn't have to put up with Phillip's company on her own.

Lee had gone to bed early because she wanted to be on her own with her thoughts. She wanted to lie and think about the kisses Brad had given her. They had certainly made her forget Phillip's and she had enjoyed them even though they might not have been important to him. It was nice to lie awake thinking about the joy of being held in Brad's arms. She wasn't kidding herself that the kisses meant anything to him and admitted that she had fallen for his charms though it was useless and she had been warned not to. So long as nobody knew that she had been stupid enough to fall in love with him it didn't matter so much.

She wondered if Mrs Palmerston would take advantage of his offer to take her back with him to Rio for a holiday and whether there was a possibility that she could go, too. It would be marvellous to travel to a country like that. She had never been farther than Paris and loved travelling by air.

Perhaps Brad had only suggested taking her to see what Phillip's reaction would be. She felt sure that Phillip had given Brad the impression that there was something between herself and him and for all she knew Brad could believe his brother and not her.

He had admitted that he had taken Phillip's girl from him and she pondered over what might have gone wrong between them, whether it was Brad's fault that it had all petered out, or Iris's. They must have had something really strong going for them for her to leave the country with him. He had been younger then, of course, and perhaps it had seemed fun to steal his brother's girl. Now he was older and would behave differently, she hoped. Phillip was worrying unnecessarily for Brad could have no intention of trying to steal her affection from him.

But what was she thinking of? She had no affection for Phillip and Brad wouldn't have to steal her away because she didn't belong to him. Perhaps Iris had felt the same way, too.

When she got down the next morning

Phillip was waiting for her, but there was no sign of Brad. 'Let's go before Brad gets up,' said Phillip. 'We don't want him tagging along with us.'

'Oh, we couldn't do that,' exclaimed Lee. 'It would look awful to go without him when he said he'd join us.'

'No need to worry,' said Brad, appearing from outside. 'I've been up ages. I couldn't sleep.'

Phillip glared at him but Brad seemed quite oblivious of his brother's displeasure. Lee couldn't take her eyes off Brad in his riding outfit. He was a fine specimen of manhood. He was wearing a cream thick knit sweater with a polo neck and she wondered if it was borrowed from Phillip or whether it was amongst the clothes he had left behind when he left so long ago. If it was Phillip's sweater she had never noticed that it suited him as it did Brad, nor could Phillip look anywhere near so dashing.

Brad chose to ride Satan, a very spirited horse, and Lee had to smile to herself. The mount suited the rider. Brad looked just a little bit wicked this morning. She knew that he was well aware that Phillip was furious because he had decided to come on this ride with them. Phillip couldn't begrudge him this pleasure. After all, his brother had done hardly anything but work since he arrived home.

Lee allowed her horse to move a little behind the men so that she could watch Brad as he rode. She could look her fill while she was behind and Phillip wouldn't notice and show his displeasure. But after a time they stopped for her to catch up, thinking they were going too fast for her.

The two men decided to have a race across the meadows and Lee said she would watch. She wasn't so good on a horse that she could enter into competition with men. She knew that neither would wish the other to win and it appeared that Brad was gaining and the horse's nose was a little in front when Phillip played a dirty trick.

He sent his horse into Brad's to slow him up and his horse nearly came a cropper. How mean Phillip could be! thought Lee angrily. He could have caused Brad to fall from the horse. They didn't continue with the race and when Lee joined them she expected to see Brad looking furious over what his brother had done, but he seemed quite unconcerned.

It was surprising how two brothers could be so different in character. Lee felt that Phillip would stoop to anything to get one over on Brad. But Brad was talking to him and laughing over something and the incident in which Phillip had put him in danger wasn't even mentioned when she reached them.

Brad looked full of exhilaration after his race with Phillip. His hair was blowing in the wind and he was thoroughly enjoying himself. Lee had never enjoyed a ride so much before. When Phillip joined her they had never made it a fun thing cantering over the fields, but Brad shouted to them and was full of life and joy. He was obviously born to an outdoor life and thoroughly enjoyed it.

He even seemed to have infused some of his *joie de vivre* into Phillip for he seemed far more animated this morning than usual. As they approached the stables again at the end of their ride Lee took off her riding-hat and her silken dark hair moved gently in the breeze. Her face was flushed with the exertion and fresh air and she was absolutely famished.

'I'm dying for my breakfast,' said Brad, coming alongside her. 'And you look so delicious I could eat you.'

Lee burst into laughter and then caught the look on Phillip's face. He was scowling and there was almost a look of evil in his expression because she was having a laugh with his brother.

'Are you hungry, too?' she asked, thinking to put him into a good mood.

'Yes,' he admitted, but he didn't

return her smile. He looked thoroughly disgruntled and she wondered how he could be like that when they'd had such an enjoyable time, the three of them.

6

There was very little work for Lee that day so she decided to take the opportunity to go and spend the day at her own home. There was no reason why she shouldn't go home every day after work was finished for she lived only a few miles away, but it suited Mrs Palmerston to have her staying with them for sometimes she would work with Lee in the evenings, or Lee would help her when she was entertaining ladies from her various groups. She supposed Mrs Palmerston was glad of her company, too, for Phillip had not been a great help to her after she'd lost her husband. It seemed he didn't have it in him to show compassion for her and yet he would be sunk without her.

It was all the more amazing to Lee, in view of his cold nature to have him suddenly showing an interest in her. An interest she didn't want and for that reason she felt she wanted to get away to her own home for a break. Another reason was to stop making a fool of herself over Brad. She found that every time she looked at him, or he at her, her knees went wobbly. No one had ever had that effect on her before. She heard of girls falling in love and doing anything for love and had thought the word was overrated, but now she knew it was not. She was in love and her thoughts were continually on Brad. Whatever she was doing he was there in her mind. He would be leaving soon and it was best that she got away from him so that his leaving wouldn't affect her so much.

But even away from him and his home she still had him constantly on her mind. He was like an obsession. She could see him on the tractor and kept thinking of the hours she spent with him ploughing in the dark by artificial light. She thought of him flying across the fields on Satan, thoroughly enjoying himself. He was older than Phillip but in some ways was more youthful. He was certainly more mature in his thinking. He would plan his working days whereas Phillip let days go by without using them to advantage.

Phillip didn't seem to realise that the responsibility of the Palmerston estate rested on him and he was not a suitable person to be in charge. He saw Brad as a threat to himself. He was afraid that Brad would try and steal Lee away and she supposed he would miss her, but not in the way he wanted her to believe, or Brad. He would miss her because she saved him hours of book work. It was doubtful whether he would be able to cope with the accounts on his own. He had no patience and if he wanted anything and Lee was not available he would wreck her filing system throwing out everything in order to find what he wanted.

Any other man would have made

himself familiar with book-keeping but Phillip ignored unpleasant things. He knew his mother would pay accounts before they became overdue and he didn't care that it was her earnings that were carrying them along at times.

Of course Lee had been aware many times that accounts were due for payment and Mrs Palmerston had seemed anxious to receive payment for articles she had had published, and then when the cheque arrived she had given a sigh of relief and the account had been paid.

Lee hadn't attached too much importance to this before. But now she understood that it must have been a great worry to her employer to know that the running of the estate depended so much on her receiving regular cheques coming in from her writing. That was no way to run an estate. Phillip hadn't bothered so long as he could go on in his own sweet way. It had been Brad who had made her aware of the state of affairs, the seriousness of the matter.

Lee stayed overnight at her own home. Her parents were glad to have her and she enjoyed being with her family for a change. She listened to all the gossip from Jane and Catherine, heard about their latest boy friends, and Mark, her wonderful brother described how he had scored a magnificent goal for his team at the weekend. 'It was a beauty!' he exclaimed.

They liked to listen to what she had to tell them about her life in the country. It wasn't so far away from her home and yet it seemed like another world to Lee and to her family. She liked being surrounded by fields and travelling along narrow little country lanes instead of being in the town where the houses were crowded in on top of each other and the streets were full of traffic so that it was a work of art to cross a road safely.

She told them about her visit to the Willoughbys and realised as she was talking about these influential people that there was a little snob appeal about being able to tell them how she had mixed with the well-to-do and had been invited to join their sports' club. And of course she talked about Brad. He was always cropping up in her conversation.

She didn't realise how much she had included him in her tales about life at the Palmerstons' until she was ready to leave home the following morning, and her mother mentioned it.

They were alone in the kitchen, everyone having gone off to work and Mrs Robson said, 'Lee, you're in love with Brad Palmerston, aren't you?'

Lee had gone red. 'Of course not,' she declared, not knowing where to look.

'Don't think I'm prying into your private life, dear,' said her mother. 'It's just that you've hardly seemed to leave him out of any of your conversations at all and your eyes seem to light up when you talk about him. I know the symptoms, love, and I'm worried because you know a man like Brad Palmerston wouldn't marry a girl from your background.'

'I don't think a girl's background would worry Brad if he were in love,' said Lee. 'But I couldn't hope for a man like him to fall in love with a girl like me. He obviously isn't the marrying type anyway for he's over thirty and it can't be because he hasn't been able to find a girl that he hasn't married. With looks and personality like his he would never be short of female company. Don't worry, Mum, I know it's no use expecting anything to come from falling in love with Brad.'

She didn't mention that his brother Phillip had proposed to her and was being a bit of a pest and that was the reason why she had escaped for a short time to come and visit her family.

Her mother gave her a hug as she was leaving and Lee told her again not to worry. 'I can look after myself, Mum,' she said.

On the way back to her employers

Lee made herself realise that Brad would be leaving England shortly and she had to face up to it. She had lost one day of his company by going home and she really ought to have stayed away until he left altogether. It would have been the wisest course, she was sure, but she could hardly tell Mrs Palmerston that she didn't want to return until Brad had gone back to Brazil.

Both Brad and Phillip were missing when she arrived at the house. Mrs Robinson told her that Mrs Palmerston had wanted to go to town on business so Phillip had taken her, and that surprised Lee because Phillip rarely ran his mother anywhere; he left that to her, but of course she hadn't been available this morning.

'Mrs Palmerston said to tell you, Lee, that there was some typing for you in the study by the typewriter.'

'Thanks,' said Lee, and after a welcome cup of coffee she went off to do it. It was yet another article so she knew her employer had been busy during her absence.

Lee liked typing Mrs Palmerston's work for her. It was more interesting than typing dull business letters and she found herself reading the article before commencing to type it out.

By lunch time she had finished typing and just as she was about to go for something to eat, Phillip and his mother returned but there was no sign of Brad and she hadn't seen him all morning. Phillip greeted her like a long lost soul and she saw his mother's eyes upon them. She hated this show of affection from Phillip because she knew it wasn't genuine. She would have hated it even more if it had been.

'Your article is ready for the post, Mrs Palmerston,' she said.

'Oh, that's good, Lee. I think I'll take a walk down to the post-box after lunch.'

'I can take it for you,' said Lee, for she knew it was a long walk to the nearest post-box.

'It will do me good to take a walk,' said Mrs Palmerston. 'I used to do a lot more walking than I do these days.'

Lee looked at her anxiously. Since she'd had that blackout Lee always felt a little concerned about her and didn't think she ought to walk so far on her own. But Phillip didn't seem concerned so perhaps there was no harm in her taking a walk. The doctor hadn't advised against it.

She thought afterwards that Phillip's mother had decided to take that walk for a purpose. It was to give Phillip and Lee a chance to talk on their own, and that must have been the reason for Brad's absence, too. They had both known that Phillip wanted to ask her something.

All through lunch he had been giving her meaningful little smiles which she had tried to ignore and he was looking very pleased with himself. As soon as they'd finished dining he suggested they went into the lounge as he wanted to talk to her. There was an air of excitement about him.

It was a nice day and she thought it would have been nice to talk out of doors but wouldn't suggest such a thing, feeling she wouldn't trust herself alone with Phillip after those horrible kisses he had forced upon her by the stables.

'We've been having some very important talks while you have been with your family,' began Phillip, when she was seated on one of the heavily brocaded chairs.

'Oh, yes,' she said, wondering how they could affect her and give cause for this intimate little talk.

'When my father died he left everything, as you know, to my mother apart from money that had been set aside especially for Brad and me. Of course it was understood that should anything happen to mother the estate would be shared equally between me and Brad.'

'Naturally,' said Lee. Hadn't Brad told her that he hadn't been cut off by his father?

'You know I have been anxious to sell off some of the land?'

Lee nodded and he went on. 'I'm fed up with having no capital to speak of. I'm not destitute, of course, but in order to marry, have a nice home and live the way I would like to live I need more than I have. A lot more. Brad and mother as you know, are not in favour of selling off the land and so Brad made an alternative suggestion to me which suits me very well.'

'Oh, yes?' Lee was interested. What could Brad have offered him?

'Instead of my selling off the land to outsiders he has suggested that I sell some of the land to him. Mother is making arrangements to have the estate transferred to Brad and me. We have been to the solicitors this morning to discuss it.'

So that was why he'd taken her to town.

'Brad is willing to buy one half of my share at a very attractive price.'

'That means he will have three-quarters of the estate to your quarter?'

'That's right.'

'Don't you object to that? After all, you are working here, not Brad.'

'My aim is to get some money instead of having to consider every penny I spend. What Brad has offered will really put me on my feet and as he says, the land will still be in the hands of the Palmerstons.'

Lee wondered if Brad thought he was on to a good thing offering to buy a half of Phillip's share or whether he really wanted to do him a good turn.

'Well, that's up to you, Phillip. It's nothing to do with me.'

'But it is. Brad is willing to do me this favour so that you and I can get married.'

'What!'

She looked at him incredulously. 'Why should Brad think I would be influenced by whether you had money or not? You didn't give him that impression, did you? That I would marry you if you had plenty of money? I hope you didn't.'

'I told him that I wasn't in a position to marry, and you knew that. He said if that was true he would buy the land from me and we could go ahead. He can't pay for the value of the land all in one go. He suggests that he lets me have a third when we get married, another third after five years and the remainder after another five years so that we'll be assured of a good life style for some time to come, and I'll still have a quarter share in the estate.

'I don't believe it!' cried Lee. 'That you could plan things like this in my absence. You know that I don't want to marry you, Phillip. What makes you think you can bribe me like this?'

'I'm not trying to bribe you,' he said, indignantly. 'I'm just telling you that now I am in a position to marry and don't tell me it isn't tempting for you to accept me now that you know you would be doing well for yourself.'

'Do you know how cold-blooded you

sound?' she asked. 'Don't you think that love comes into it when a couple discuss marriage?'

'Well, all that would follow, naturally.'

'In other words you are admitting that you don't love me, but that in time you might?'

'I have had you on my mind quite a lot, lately, Lee,' he said, looking hurt. 'I'm fonder of you than I imagined.'

'I think you've only been interested in me since Brad arrived and you thought he might be.'

'Does there have to be a reason why I want to marry you?'

'Why, of course there has to be a reason! Your reason is because you want to get your hands on that money Brad has offered you. But the only possible reason I can see for marriage is because you love that person and she loves you.'

'You have to go into marriage with your eyes wide open,' he said. 'I've thought about it a lot. You aren't the type who would squander a fortune away in no time, you are too level-headed for that. This would be a good match for you, Lee, and I want to marry you. I'd be good to you,' he added, almost as an afterthought.

Lee doubted that he would. He hadn't shown much sympathy and affection towards his mother although she had been distressed and lonely since losing her husband. If she thwarted Phillip in any way, Lee knew he could be quite ruthless as she had discovered when he had forced those punishing kisses on her. He would be worse if she married him, she felt sure. He made it look as if he was doing her a favour in asking her.

'I'm sorry, Phillip, but the answer is the same as before. I am not in love with you and I couldn't marry you just for the money. Thank you for asking me, but there it is.'

'So you wouldn't put yourself out to help me take advantage of Brad's offer? You know how much it means to me.'

'I know that it means more to you than marrying me does. If you could still have the money from Brad without marriage to me I don't think you'd be all that keen for me to be your wife. You know lots of more eligible women, anyway.'

'Yes, I do,' he said. 'Perhaps you're right. It's only since I've seen Brad eyeing you that I've felt I wanted you for myself. And I do want you, Lee.'

He had a most unfortunate way of expressing himself, she thought, feeling a little sorry for him. Talking about Brad eyeing her made her feel like some cheap little piece being offered for sale.

'How can Brad have any interest in me if he has made this offer to you so that you can marry me?' she asked him.

That was the thought that had been at the back of her mind all the time since Phillip had put his proposal forward. She loved Brad but he was making plans for her to marry his brother. Perhaps he thought she would make an ideal wife for Phillip because she would keep all the accounts in order, wouldn't squander his money, and all that would be to Brad's advantage. He couldn't be here all the time to keep everything working as he would wish. She wanted to get away from Phillip and cry her heart out.

'Lee, you're happy here,' Phillip began to argue. 'You get on well with my mother, you know you'd be unhappy if you had to leave.'

'Yes, I would, Phillip,' she said, 'and so I beg of you not to go on. You were talking of buying a house so I would have to leave in that case and I'd rather not. I'm contented as I am. I don't want to be married.'

She was appalled when he began to beg her to accept his proposal. He crouched down beside her and pleaded with her. 'Don't turn me down, Lee, please. It's so important to me. I was sure you'd want to marry me when you heard my news. I've been dying to get you on your own so that I could tell you all about it.'

His face was close to hers and his eyes were so beseeching as he pleaded with her to accept him that she felt dreadful. She believed now that he desperately wanted her to marry him, but she couldn't marry him out of pity, or to do him a favour. She had to think of herself. Her whole life was at stake and she knew she couldn't bear to spend the rest of her life married to a man she didn't love.

She rose in order to move away from him and that pleading expression on his face and as she did so he caught her in his arms and tried to kiss her. 'No, Phillip, please!' she cried. 'It's no use. It's really no use.'

At that he lost his temper and pulled her close to force her to kiss him and at this display of savagery she knew she'd done the right thing. She pulled herself away and it took all her effort. He caught her again and this time there was no pleading or gentleness; he shook her because she didn't want him and then gave her a stinging blow across the face.

She looked at him aghast. 'Phillip!' she cried, and tears began to fall. 'You are a disgusting bully. No girl would be safe married to you. And now you've made my position here so unthinkable I shall have to leave and that was the last thing I wanted to do.'

'Yes, you leave,' he shouted. 'You're an ungrateful little devil. Who do you think you are to turn down a man in my position?'

'Let me go!' she cried.

But he wouldn't let her get past him to leave him and she stood there with tears streaming down her face.

'Don't cry, Lee,' he said, his voice and attitude changing. 'I've gone about everything the wrong way, haven't I? It really would mean a lot to me if you would change your mind.'

'You can't expect me to want you, Phillip, when you can be so ruthless.'

'I don't mean to be. I haven't got

Brad's way with the girls. I don't know how to go about charming them until they'll do anything for me as they will for him. You like Brad, don't you?'

'Of course I do and I've always liked you until you've let me see how awful you can be.'

'Give me another chance. Let me show you that I could take care of you and make you happy.'

She hid her face from him and couldn't look at him.

He tried once again to draw her into his arms. 'Lee, we've had such serious talks, Mother, Brad and I, and I'll look such a fool when I have to tell them that you won't have me even with all that money.'

'Phillip, don't make me feel so bad about refusing you.'

'But I feel bad about it.'

'You should look for a girl who will love you as a wife should love her husband, Phillip.'

'What is it about me that you don't like? I'll be different.'

'Do you want me to tell you the honest truth?'

'Yes.'

'Well, I don't think you could put someone else before yourself. It is very important for a girl to feel that she means everything to the one she marries and you have never made me feel important to you. You think I should be grateful to you for asking me to be your wife. I would have been grateful if your attitude had been different. I might even have fallen in love with you for I've been working at your home long enough, but you have always kept your distance until now, and then you decided you wanted to marry me and that I should fall in with your wishes just like that. You could have said that you'd be grateful if I accepted you, but no, according to you it was I who should show gratitude.'

'I'd be grateful. Honestly.'

'No courting, no trying to win my affection, no convincing me that you really care, and showing a vicious streak when you can't have your own way.'

'You make me sound a detestable creature.'

'You have to convince people that you're not.'

'I suppose that means that you do think I'm detestable?'

'You can't say that your behaviour hasn't been. Let me go, Phillip. We aren't going to get anywhere talking like this. Thanks for your proposal but I can't accept it and I suppose you still want me to leave?'

'That's up to you,' he said, and then made way for her to pass him.

'Very well. I think I'll wait for your mother to return and then I'll go.'

'You're being stupid.'

'Perhaps I am, but I should feel very uncomfortable working here now so it would be best if I left.'

She ran past him and up to her room. There she sat on the bed to reflect on what had just happened and thought that in a way she almost hated Phillip, yet she couldn't help feeling sorry for him. Why should that be? He had behaved abominably. It hadn't been a nice proposal. No man in his right mind would expect a girl to accept a proposal of that nature, pointing out that it would be a good thing for her to be given the opportunity to marry a man in his position. Conceited creature. She supposed some avaricious girl would have been tempted, but she didn't think that the girl who married Phillip would be generously treated.

He obviously didn't see himself as others saw him and she hoped it would do him good to tell him why she hadn't accepted him. As for Brad, she began to think he was as despicable as his brother. He had known very well that she had been upset by his brother's behaviour the other evening and yet he had deliberately discussed making it possible for Phillip to marry her by offering to let him have some capital. A fine opinion he must have of her, too, to think that the thought of Phillip's money would tempt her to marry him in spite of her dislike of him.

The thought that Brad could do that to her was even more upsetting than anything Phillip had said or done. She wouldn't have believed him capable of making such arrangements with Phillip. She even felt a little bitter towards Mrs Palmerston, too, for she had been in on it all, she was sure, for hadn't she gone out in order to give Phillip a chance to talk to Lee herself?

She got up and began to pack her belongings, watching as she did so from the window for Mrs Palmerston's return from posting her letter. Even that had been arranged carefully. A letter to post was a good excuse to go out. And where was Brad? she wondered. He had taken off, too, probably too ashamed to face her knowing he had manoeuvred this situation. What a cheek on the part of the three of them to have discussed her future while she had been away for little over a day. She felt very hurt about it all.

As she put her clothes into her trunk

she couldn't help feeling sad that such an enjoyable job had come to an end. She would never get another as good as this one had been. This house had been more like home to her over the past two years than her own home with her parents had been and she knew she was going to miss it. She would miss the gorgeous views from the windows, her horse-riding, the walks across the fields, miss going with Mrs Palmerston to her meetings and typing out her interesting articles.

And worse than anything was the hurt that Brad had shown so clearly how little she meant to him. Of course she hadn't believed for one moment that any depth of feeling could develop between the two of them, but she had liked his company and had thought he liked hers.

Then she thought of the way Brad had kissed her in order to wipe out Phillip's earlier kisses and he had told her it was nice. That was an instance in which she should have heeded Phillip's advice. He had warned her not to fall for Brad's charm but she had done and now she had to pay for it.

Perhaps she would be able to get away from the house before he returned from wherever he had disappeared to. She felt she couldn't face him ever again. But she had to see Mrs Palmerston before she left and from her bedroom window she watched anxiously for her to put in an appearance.

7

Everything was packed into Lee's cases by the time Mrs Palmerston returned. She came walking slowly towards the house after her long walk and Lee could see that she was not a young woman any more. Not being aware that she was being watched she allowed herself to sag a little and her footsteps were not so sharp. In company she made an effort to appear alert and full of life.

It was hateful having to go down and tell her she was leaving but there was nothing else for it. It would be embarrassing to have to meet Phillip constantly for she didn't know how he would behave towards her now that she had definitely turned him down. It was stupid of him to have led his brother and his mother to believe that she would accept him for she hadn't given him the right to do that.

Lee went down and met Mrs Palmerston in the hall and immediately noticed the anxious look on the older woman's face as she met Lee's eyes. 'I can see that Phillip was mistaken, Lee. You haven't accepted him, have you?'

'No, I'm sorry. He didn't take it very well, either.'

'Oh, dear!'

'I told him that it would be best if I left and he agreed, though later he did tell me to please myself. But I must go.'

'Oh, no,' said Mrs Palmerston. 'I can't let you go, Lee.'

'But how could I stay in the circumstances?'

'Don't be hasty. Ask Mrs Robinson to bring some coffee into the sitting-room, there's a dear. I could do with a drink.'

Lee went to ask Mrs Robinson to bring the coffee in, feeling that her employer looked as if she could do with something stronger than coffee.

When she joined her in the sitting-room she was slumped wearily in an easy chair.

'You shouldn't have gone to the post, Mrs Palmerston,' said Lee, regarding her in concern. 'I knew it would be too much for you.'

'It's not that, Lee. I've been so worried lately what with one thing and another. Phillip isn't happy, as you know. He's been discontented for a long time and I thought Brad and I might have come up with a solution. Well, Phillip seemed sure enough that you would be glad to accept his proposal.'

'Did you think I would, Mrs Palmerston?'

'I thought you might. I told you before I would have liked you to be my daughter-in-law. We get on so well, Lee. It would have made me very happy, and it would be nice to have at least one of my sons married. It would be nice to have grandchildren. Most of my friends talk about their grandchildren and I always envy them.'

'And did Brad think I would accept him?'

'I don't know,' said his mother. 'He and Phillip had been talking and the next thing I knew he had made this offer to help you both. You and Phillip.'

Lee was very tempted to tell her that Brad knew very well she wouldn't agree to marry Phillip for she had told him about those hateful kisses and had made it clear to him that she had no great liking for his brother. But it was he who had made the suggestion to buy land from Phillip so that he could marry Lee. Did he believe she would marry a man for money? He obviously did or he wouldn't have made the offer to Phillip. She couldn't explain to his mother that she had told Brad how much she disliked his brother's behaviour because a mother wouldn't want to hear anything bad about her son.

'Phillip has never tried to win my

affection,' said Lee. 'He was quite indifferent towards me until Brad came home. Although he took me out and often went horse-riding with me he always treated me with great reserve. He never gave me any reason to believe that he cared for me and I don't think he does. I'm sure the only reason he suddenly began to take an interest in me was because he thought Brad might take to me and then he decided he wanted me himself.'

'Perhaps so,' said his mother. 'He has always been jealous of Brad. I suppose a younger son often is. He saw Brad capable of doing many things that he couldn't do and Brad also had a way with girls that Phillip didn't have. The worst blow was when Brad took Iris away with him. That was an awful thing to do to his brother.'

Lee told herself once more that neither of the Palmerston sons were very nice, and yet their mother was so likeable. She deserved more happiness in life. Now Lee was going to have to leave her. She hoped it wouldn't upset her too much.

Mrs Robinson brought in the coffee and said it looked like rain, and Lee saw that dark clouds were gathering. She poured the coffee and handed her employer a cup. Mrs Palmerston took it thankfully. 'You were right, Lee,' she said, 'it was a long jaunt to the post office, I feel exhausted.'

Lee sipped her coffee and looked at Mrs Palmerston sympathetically and Mrs Palmerston took in Lee's tearstained face. 'You don't have to go, Lee,' she said. 'Everything will blow over and you'll forget that Phillip proposed to you and that you had to refuse.'

Lee couldn't tell Phillip's mother that her son could be rather ruthless and that she couldn't forget.

'Let me have a word with Phillip,' said his mother. 'Where is he, by the way?'

'He must have gone out in a temper, I suppose.'

'Not in a temper, surely. Maybe upset over your refusal, but not in a temper, Lee.'

'He was angry with me.'

Lee felt he would have gone out in a temper, rather than in sorrow. He didn't like being rejected. She was sure he didn't care enough about her to be upset; he was much more likely to be furious because she had spoiled his chance of getting his hands on some money. He had let her know that he regarded it as doing her a favour to ask her to be his wife.

Lee would admit that the Palmerstons were higher up the social scale than the Robsons, but she didn't want it pointing out to her as Phillip had done. She was not a social climber, was quite contented with her status in life, and resented being told that she would be doing well for herself if she accepted Phillip's proposal. For one thing she didn't believe she would be doing well for herself because he wasn't her type at all and if she'd married him she could imagine that he would constantly remind her that he'd done her a favour. He was a ruthless man. He would never consider her happiness; he was too selfish. If he'd been a nice person and she had been in love with him it wouldn't have mattered if he hadn't a penny so long as he was prepared to work to provide for them, but Phillip considered himself above working for his living, apparently.

She had to admit that Brad was different in that respect although she was still furious with him for plotting with Phillip to enable him to get Lee for his wife. Brad didn't mind getting stuck into work and she didn't feel he was a snob, either. He had never made her feel that he was superior to herself as Phillip did.

She knew she was going over and over again in her mind all that had happened because she simply couldn't dismiss it that easily. It would take her a long time to forget what had happened this afternoon.

'I think I'd better go now,' said Lee, putting her coffee cup down and rising. 'I'm terribly sorry and upset about having to leave, Mrs Palmerston. I've loved working for you.'

Mrs Palmerston rose, too, and caught Lee's hand. 'I know you've loved your job. We've worked together very well, dear, and I wish I could persuade you not to go.'

'Who's talking of going,' came a voice in the doorway, and Lee coloured when she saw it was Brad. She didn't want to see him any more than she wanted to see Phillip, so she turned on him with an icy glare and then pushed past him to go up for her cases. She left his mother to explain that she was leaving.

In her room Lee took a deep breath so that she could calmly take her cases downstairs and leave without a fresh bout of tears. She had been living here as if it were her own home for a long time and had accumulated lots of stuff so it would take her several journeys downstairs to get it all to her car. She hoped no one would interfere with her leaving and wished she'd got away before Brad came in.

She lifted the first heavy case from the bed and was about to turn with it when she found it lifted from her hand and thrown back on the bed. 'You can't leave my mother,' he snapped.

'Oh, can't I?' she cried, angrily. 'You and your brother talking to me the way you do. I hate you both.'

'From that I gather that Phillip gave you a bad time when you refused him? Well, I'm not Phillip and I don't want you to put me in the same category. I've never done anything to hurt you and you know it.'

'Oh, no! You wouldn't do anything to hurt me,' she cried. 'Only offered Phillip a good hand out if he could get me to marry him.'

'We won't go into that now,' he said. 'I'm worried about my mother, Lee. Can't you see how upset and down she is? I don't know what she'd do without you. I gather you've been a great help to her since my father died, more help than either Phillip or I could have been, and she cares about you a lot. You wouldn't hurt her, Lee?'

'I suppose it doesn't matter if I'm hurt,' she retorted.

'Of course it does,' he said. 'It matters about you and Mother and Phillip.'

'You knew I wouldn't accept him. Why did you boost his expectations by telling him he could have that money in order to get my consent to marry him?'

'That's another story. I'll explain everything, but at this moment I want you to go down and tell Mother you're not going.'

'Oh, anyone could have helped your mother as I did. There are plenty of other typists and book-keepers about.'

'Please, Lee.'

She looked at him with tears once again streaming down her face and she had tried so hard not to cry any more.

She had hated Brad but as soon as he spoke like that it was her undoing. He caught her in his arms and held her close but he made no attempt to kiss her, just comforted her as he would anyone who was upset.

'Come on. You go down to Mother and I'll go and find Phillip. He'll be upset, Lee. He did think he had a good chance with you when you knew he would be well off.'

'He gets savage when he can't have his own way.'

'That's a sign of immaturity. He has to grow up. Children throw tantrums when they can't get their own way.'

She sniffed and he handed her his handkerchief. 'Here, give a good blow,' he smiled, 'and come downstairs with me.'

'I can't go on working here with Phillip,' she insisted.

'Perhaps you won't have to. I've been trying to persuade mother to come to Rio with me for a holiday. She'll be bound to want you to do some typing for her because she'll be writing about everything she sees. She's always been a writer, she couldn't give it up even on a holiday.'

Rio de Janeiro! Never in her wildest dreams had Lee imagined she would go so far from home. It was very tempting to accept that offer. She dried her eyes and he assured her that she looked fine before taking her hand and persuading her to go down to his mother.

Mrs Palmerston smiled when she saw Lee hand in hand with Brad. 'Has he persuaded you not to go?' she asked.

'I don't know,' said Lee.

'Yes, you do,' said Brad. 'You're not leaving my mother and that's that.'

It was all right for him. He was thinking about his mother not herself.

He marched off out presumably to search for Phillip and his mother began to laugh. 'You know I rather like having Brad back. He's bossy but he means well. His intentions are good.'

Lee laughed, too. 'He says that you are going to Brazil and that I am going with you to do your typing there.'

'I wouldn't be at all surprised,' said his mother and Lee thought she looked much better than she'd done when she returned from the post office. Brad had had that effect on her. But Lee still didn't understand what he was up to. He said he would explain why he had offered Phillip so much money on condition that she became his wife. Well, that would need a lot of explaining.

It was a long time before Brad returned with Phillip who had obviously been drinking. Lee wouldn't have believed he could be so affected because she had turned him down, and then she told herself not to be so stupid. He was not affected because she had turned him down but because he wouldn't be able to have all those thousands of pounds Brad had promised him for the land now that he wasn't getting married because he wouldn't be needing it desperately.

Brad took Phillip upstairs and Lee

looked at Mrs Palmerston with a wry look on her face. 'I do feel dreadful,' she said.

'He'll get over it,' said his mother, but Lee knew she was bound to be concerned about her son. In the circumstances it was nice of her to want Lee to stay with her even though she had upset Phillip.

When Brad came down he joined Lee and his mother. 'It's no use trying to talk to him in his present state,' he said, 'but I gather he's very disappointed that he will not have the wealth he expected. As soon as he's all right I'll let him know that it doesn't make any difference whether he marries or not, I am still prepared to pay him for half of his share if that's what he wants. I offered it to him in order that he could feel in a position to get married, and as far as I'm concerned he can still have it even though he doesn't get married. But he'd be a fool to have the money and waste it.'

Why couldn't he have told Phillip

that before? Lee asked herself. It would have saved her having to refuse his proposal of marriage.

She wondered if Brad was willing to buy some of Phillip's share in order to gain control over the running of the estate, but he stemmed those suspicions by saying, 'If he ever wants to buy back his share it will be okay by me. I know at the moment he is just frustrated because he has no capital to speak of. But he should have some money, shouldn't he, Mother? He has had sums of money left to him and given to him in the past and yet he doesn't seem to have any now. He reckons he is broke.'

'Perhaps he's been gambling as his father used to,' said Mrs Palmerston.

'I shouldn't like to think I was letting him have money to indulge in gambling,' said Brad. 'I'm afraid to gamble myself. It can be like a disease that gets a hold on you. Dad squandered far too much money on the race courses but I've kept my gambling strictly to business ventures and have never taken a gamble without a great deal of thought and a certainty that I'm on a winner.'

'Try to instil that into Phillip,' said his mother. 'We don't want to see him broke again soon after he's received the money from you.'

'I expect a lot will go that way if gambling has got a hold on him. Dad was to blame for that. But for that reason I agreed to pay him the money over a period of fifteen years so that he can't squander the lot as soon as he has it.'

Lee thought of her own father. A pound spent in gambling on the Derby or Grand National and a few shillings a week on the football coupons was as far as he went and her mother grumbled about that sometimes, telling him he was throwing his money away. She hadn't been so bad since her father won a couple of hundred pounds a year ago, but gambling was frowned upon as a general rule in her family.

Brad began to tell them of his travels in South America, presumably to try and get his mother to go over there for a holiday. He lived in Rio de Janeiro in an air-conditioned house he told them. 'It has a swimming pool,' he mentioned, proudly. He had made lots of friends out there and Lee wondered how many of them were females. Perhaps he had a woman sharing his home with him, but he didn't include any girls in his conversation.

'I went on a journey into the Amazon forests,' he said, and began to describe what it was like in the jungle. 'There is no King of the Amazonian jungle as there is in the African jungle where the lion is king. There are so many different species of animal that no particular one can get the upper hand. The spotted jaguar might be considered lord of the jungle but he gets attacked by giant boa constrictors, alligators, or the fire ant.'

Mrs Palmerston shuddered at the thought of snakes and insects. 'How horrible,' she said. 'You're not making me want to come to see you in Brazil.'

Brad laughed. 'I'm not suggesting taking you into the jungle, Mother. Rio de Janeiro is the cultural centre of the country and it is considered to have one of the world's most beautiful natural harbours, surrounded by low mountain ranges. And, of course, you've heard of the Corcovado peak which is the site of a colossal statue of Christ. It's most impressive.'

'Yes, I've heard of that,' said Mrs Palmerston and Lee together.

'But the climate's terrible isn't it?' said Mrs Palmerston. 'Hot and humid, most unpleasant.'

'I've survived,' said Brad.

'And you've got a wonderful tan,' said Lee.

'You think it's wonderful, like me?' he asked, playfully.

She remembered that she was angry with him for encouraging Phillip to ask her to marry him when he knew very well it was the furthest thought from her mind and so she did not return his smile, or answer his question.

'Think about it, Mother,' he said. 'I'd like you to come and see where I live. You needn't stay long if you don't like it.'

'It would cost a lot to go to Rio, Brad,' she said. 'I couldn't possibly afford it.'

'Yes, you could,' he said. 'But I'm not asking you to buy the tickets; I'll buy one for you, and one for Lee. I've done extremely well in South America. Huge industries are starting up there and I've met the right people. I'm in partnerships in a chemical concern with a South American scientist who had all the qualifications needed to start a research laboratory but not the capital, and it's a great success. And again, as I've told you, I have been acting as a business consultant helping people to get their affairs in order, or putting them wise when they are just starting up over there. I've had my eye to business.'

'How have you become qualified to advise business people?' she asked.

'Easy,' he laughed. 'When people bring problems to me I tell them to let me think them over and then I seek the advice of experts which I then pass on to them. And in that way I have learned a lot so that I have become something of an expert myself.'

'You didn't have a great deal of money to start with,' said his mother. 'How could you put money into a research laboratory?'

'I went to see Gran and Grandpa before I left and Grandpa let me have some money to start me off. He had more faith in me than you and Dad did. I didn't ask for it, never thought of having anything from them but they both insisted, and with what I had of my own I was able to get started. I didn't squander money as Phillip did. I've been able to let Grandpa have the money back that he loaned to me and he knows that it's thanks to him that I've become prosperous.

Anyone in South America with money to invest can become prosperous for there are great strides being made in industry at the moment.'

His mother was quiet. 'Gran and Grandpa never said anything about lending money to you,' she said.

'No. They said they wouldn't mention it to anyone. They knew I was considered the black sheep of the family and that everyone would think they were mad for helping me out and that I'd squander the money, but I didn't,' he said, with pride.

He went off upstairs to see how Phillip was. Mrs Palmerston looked at Lee. 'I feel dreadfully ashamed about the way Brad's father and I treated him, you know.'

'Perhaps you did him a favour in the long run,' said Lee. 'He left home and has apparently made himself a fortune.'

'You're a good girl,' said her employer. 'You always make me feel I haven't been so bad after all. Brad has shown no bitterness towards me or Phillip since he came back. He has been annoyed about the way Phillip has neglected things, but he's been prepared to give a helping hand to get us prosperous as he thinks we ought to be.'

'You are not keen to go to Brazil to see his home, are you?' asked Lee, sensing that his mother had not been over enthusiastic about the idea while he had been talking about it.

'Perhaps I ought to go. If he is proud of his home out there it seems rather mean not to go and see it after being invited.'

'It does,' said Lee. 'You might feel he was mean if he hadn't invited you. If he marries and settles there he will naturally expect you to visit him from time to time.'

'I don't want him to live so far away permanently.'

'I can understand that,' said Lee.

'Do you want to go out there, Lee?'

'I should be telling lies if I said I didn't,' said Lee. 'It sounds marvellous to me and I'd never get another chance to go so far from home. I'm sure I'd love it but it's not for me to decide.'

'What about things here? We can't leave Phillip to manage things here all on his own.'

'Why not?' asked Brad, returning to the room. 'It would do him the world of good to have to fend for himself for a bit. He will have no one to turn to to pay overdue bills for him and it would go against the grain for him to have to dig into that capital I'm prepared to let him have in order to have to pay bills when the money is not forthcoming from the estate. It hasn't done him any favours, Mum, knowing that you were there all the time to help him out of his difficulties. Let him stand on his own two feet.'

'I dread to think what would happen if he was left on his own.'

'It won't be for long,' said Brad. 'A lot of the work has been completed. I've given him a lot of ideas, suggested that he increases his livestock, breeds from pedigree cattle. It's up to him to prove that he's capable. He might try out my suggestions when I'm not there, whereas pride might make him ignore them while I'm around. He won't have anyone to blame if he fails. And if he does we'll have to come back and pick up the pieces and start all over again.'

His mother was still doubtful and Brad said, 'Mother, he's had you all along. For two years I've been on my own. Can't you spare a little time for me?'

Before she could answer, Phillip joined them looking pale and rather sullen, but he showed no surprise at seeing Lee still there, nor did he pass any unpleasant remarks to her.

Apparently Brad had already told him he was prepared to let him have the money although he was not to be married and over dinner he said, 'Mother and Lee are coming to Brazil with me for a holiday, Phillip.'

It was like Brad to make a statement

like that without waiting to see if they really were willing to go with him.

Phillip looked at his mother and then at Lee. 'How long shall you be away?' he asked, accepting Brad's statement quite calmly.

Seeing that he was putting up no opposition his mother turned to Brad. 'How long, do you think?' she asked.

'A journey of that distance is expensive,' he said. 'You might as well have your money's worth. Six months I should say, at the least.'

'Six months!' exclaimed Phillip.

'That's not long,' said Brad. 'Give you a chance to show your mettle. See if you can make bumper profits out of the land this year.'

'You think I couldn't,' he said, giving Brad a nasty look.

'I think you could if you wanted to,' said Brad.

'Well, clear off, all of you,' he said, in a sullen mood.

'That's just what we're going to do,' said Brad, and Lee felt a thrill run through her. She couldn't believe it. A trip to Rio de Janeiro. She had been so upset a short time ago and now she was going with Brad and his mother to the other side of the world and she could hardly contain her excitement. It was wonderful.

8

After three weeks in Rio de Janeiro, Lee and Mrs Palmerston were beginning to cope with the humidity. Lee found herself taking numerous showers to cool down and was glad to walk barefooted on the cool tiles in Brad's house.

Brad lived in a smart house with beautifully set out gardens in a very exclusive part of Rio past the Gavea golf course. There was a shanty town on the hill while the grand houses were on the flat. The contrast between the dwelling houses of the rich and the poor was great, and Lee couldn't help thinking that all over the world there was always this difference between people. Some had all they desired, others had very little, just enough to survive.

Brad had plunged into work almost as soon as he arrived here. The chemical laboratory he had told them about was in São Paulo, some two hundred and fifty miles to the east. He took them with him on one occasion by jet. Often he caught an early morning plane and was back again for dinner in the evening.

He explained to them on the journey that São Paulo had sudden swings in temperature. 'It can be terribly hot,' he said, 'and then miserably cold in the space of twenty-four hours. All well set homes need central heating as well as air conditioning.'

Brad was eager for them to see as much as possible and told them about each place they visited. 'They have summer rainstorms which can flood the city and sweep homes away, and that happens quite regularly, it's not a rare occasion.'

Neither Mrs Palmerston nor Lee were prepared for the immensity of the city and Brad told them of its importance as the largest city in Brazil with great commercial influence.

'The water that falls on this plateau,' he told them, 'drains westwards, flowing past Buenos Aires, and the Brazilians built some modest dams which have created two huge lakes, Guarapiringa and Rio Grande reservoir. The water was taken through the lip of the escarpment with a clear fall of over two thousand feet to power stations below, and this gives almost limitless reserves of cheap power. Of course, that accounts for the amazing development of São Paulo.'

Lee loved to listen to Brad talking, so full of enthusiasm and so knowledgeable. He didn't explain these things to them in a pompous way as Phillip would have done. As the plane banked to come into the airport two miles from the city centre they had a glimpse of the city's Manhattan, a skyscraping concrete core rising high above the city's exhalations, and in the background were the mountains.

'You can get English food quite easily here,' said Brad, breaking into Lee's thoughts. 'The language is still Brazilian Portuguese but you will find English is spoken a lot. You'll have no difficulty in making yourselves understood and you can buy French bread rolls, order bacon and eggs, or egg and chips.'

He took them to lunch but then had to leave them for the rest of the day to amuse themselves. They walked round the numerous shops just waiting until he could rejoin them and then they were both glad to return to Rio. Lee was enjoying this holiday immensely and the best part of all was having so much of Brad's company, with his mother, too, of course, but for all that he often made her feel he was explaining something exclusively to her and she would meet his deep blue eyes and feel a thrill run through her.

Often Mrs Palmerston preferred to stay in in the evening and didn't mind at all if Brad took Lee out. They would do their best to persuade her to accompany them but she would say, 'Oh, go on, and leave me in peace. I don't mind my own company now and again and I get tired with too much sight seeing.'

They were afraid to be too persistent. The climate could be tiring to young people let alone older ones but she seemed well and there were no more signs of a blackout like the one she had experienced in England.

'I'm sure mother was suffering from mental strain,' Brad told Lee. 'I'm glad you wrote to tell me about that blackout. I would have gone home to see her sooner but as I told you, at the time Dad died I was ill with a fever and afterwards I had the feeling my arrival back home might be misconstrued. Phillip and Mother might have got the idea I was aiming to try and take control of things as the eldest son.'

'Do you regret very much those two years away from home?'

'Being away from Mother, yes, especially when she needed someone, but otherwise no. There are great opportunities over here if you have some capital to invest and I had some so I was very lucky.'

'I wonder if Phillip is pulling his socks up as you hoped he would,' said Lee.

'He's a fool if he doesn't,' said Brad. 'He's been given every chance.'

Lee was glad to have Brad drive her in Rio. She would have been scared to drive herself for the standard of driving seemed atrocious to her. Horns were blasted, drivers changed lanes without warning and it was nothing to see a car coming down on the oncoming lane and avoid accidents by the skin of their teeth.

It amused Brad to see how tense Lee was in this sort of traffic. He had become used to it. 'It's every man for himself,' he told her with a grin.

He took her to meet friends of his and the tendency was to drink a lot which is usual in hot countries. 'If you want to enjoy many of the recreational facilities,' he told her, 'you have to join a club. I've become a member of one which means I can take advantage of all the facilities.'

Boating and water ski-ing were very popular and though Lee watched Brad water ski-ing she couldn't be persuaded to have a go herself. But the beaches were a never ending source of pleasure to her. Mrs Palmerston wasn't always keen to go to the beach but she didn't object to Lee going as much as she liked. It seemed that the beaches of Leme, Copacabana and Ipanema were always crowded. The Brazilians loved to 'fall in the water', as they called it. She was sure there were no more friendly people in the world than the Brazilians and they adored children. You could see young men of sixteen or seventeen playing with little children, demonstrating their fascination with them.

Lee learned to say *bom dia* (good morning) *boa tarde* (good afternoon) and *boa noite* for good evening or goodnight. Cheerio was *até logo*. Brad taught her to use these expressions and a few others, 'I won't tell you too many at once,' he said, 'Learn a little at a time.'

When he took her out for a meal or amongst his friends she would use the appropriate expression feeling rather self-conscious but Brad told her that people in other countries like to know that the British are willing to have a go at their language and understood when they made mistakes. 'They'll even correct you, but it's only so that you will use their language more.'

Even when Mrs Palmerston accompanied them, Lee would often find her hand taken by Brad and he would hold on to her as if she was someone special to him. And occasionally he would give her a kiss and she was sure he had no idea the effect he had upon her. She wanted him to hold her tight and kiss her more passionately, but this didn't happen and she knew it was because he wasn't in love with her as she was with him.

Amongst his friends there were often

charming young girls with whom Brad would fool and have fun and Lee would find herself wondering if one of those were special to Brad. Sometimes his secretary would ring him at home and once Lee had answered the phone and discovered that the girl had a very pleasing voice and sounded rather nice. Perhaps she was the one Brad would marry eventually. That he was in a position to marry was obvious for he already possessed a lovely home with a young Brazilian girl, Teresa, to cook for him and keep his house neat and tidy.

Although Brad put his work first he did find time to take his mother and Lee out quite frequently after the first few days of putting in extra time to make up for being away in England. He took them to the botanical gardens, and they had tea in the tea gardens. They saw the floodlit, outstretched arms of the statue of Christ on the top of the Corcovado Peak, and wherever they went Mrs Palmerston took her camera and made notes. Brad took some good photographs for her, too. It would all make interesting material for articles when she got back to England.

She also made notes of all the legends she could learn about and here Teresa was a great help. She was only too pleased to relate all the legends she knew. Country people in particular, she told them, had strange superstitions. 'They believe it is bad luck to start climbing stairs with the left foot. They do not tread in anyone's shadow and would never look over their shoulder when walking alone in the wilds. To do so would bring an eerie feeling of spookiness and an attack from behind.'

Lee was busy taking all her stories down in shorthand. Brooms should be left in an upright position unless owners wished to get rid of unwelcome guests and then the broom should be placed upside down behind the door.

These superstitions were no more strange than some from Britain that

Mrs Palmerston and Lee told Teresa, and her dark brown eyes would be full of surprise and interest.

She then went on to tell them that in their country it was believed that a huge man-monster lived in the jungle. He was called Mapinguari and was covered with red hair. Men's heads were his favourite food. He caused his victims to faint by breathing his fetid breath on them and then tore them to pieces in razor-like claws. Bullets could not kill him unless fired exactly through the navel.

A hobgoblin called Sacy-Pereré was a mischievous gnome well known in Brazilian legend. He was supposed to have one eye, one leg and to be the size of a small boy. He wore a red cap and had an unlit pipe in his mouth. Passers-by were to be wary if he stopped them and asked for a light because he was a troublemaker and capable of devilish tricks. If country people found their horses jaded in the morning and their manes all knotted they knew it was caused by Sacy-Pereré who had borrowed their horses for night rides and knotted their manes in order to hang on.

There was supposed to be a phantom cowboy who appeared on ranches when the round-up and branding were taking place. He rode a decrepit horse but could ride dozens of miles in a matter of minutes. Powerful bulls obeyed him. Women pined for him but the mysterious cowpuncher refused their advances. He could defeat his competitors in every other way including eating and drinking and after collecting his pay he disappeared only to reappear shortly afterwards on another ranch which could be a hundred and fifty miles away.

Many Indian legends had survived and they found a charming one in connection with the berries of the guaraná plant which contain guaranine which is an alkaloid nerve-stimulant said to be good for the health. It was used in the manufacture of Guarana, a soft drink which is a popular drink in Brazil and is also exported.

'Legend has it,' Brad told them, 'that many years ago a husband and wife of the Maué Indians had a son who brought great prosperity to the tribe. He was treated with great respect by the tribe because if any of them became ill, their aches and pains were cured by the young boy, and also the tribe always found plenty of food to eat because of him.'

'They are great believers in miracle cures in this country, aren't they?' said his mother.

'They are,' said Brad, and continued. 'It was said that an evil spirit called Jarupari was jealous of young Maué and one day when the boy was climbing a tree to pick fruit Jaruparí turned himself into a snake and attacked him. The Indians found the young boy dead on the ground with his eyes open and serene. They were overcome with grief but as they stood around him a ray suddenly appeared in the sky and touched the ground near them. The mother of the dead boy announced that their god Tupá had come to earth to console the tribe. The god ordered them to pluck out the boy's eyes and plant them in the ground and from them would grow a wonderful plant which would not only feed the Maué Indians but would cure their sicknesses as well.'

'Strange that the evil spirit turned into a snake,' said Lee. 'We associate a serpent with evil, too.'

'That's right,' said Brad. 'Well, the Indians obeyed the god, the good one, and plucked out the eyes of the young boy which were planted and watered by the tears of the Indians. Older members of the tribe remained behind to see what would happen. A plant soon grew in the plot and was carefully tended by the tribe and soon afterwards berries appeared on the plant and they looked exactly like the eyes of the child. This plant was the guaraná and the berries were the secret food and remedy given by the god Tupá to the Maué Indians.'

Mrs Palmerston loved collecting legends such as this and got Lee to type them out for her on Brad's typewriter. Lee knew that films would be shown back home to the womens' groups and the legends recounted.

Brad's mother had taken yards of film during her stay so far and was adding to her collection all the time. She was looking happy and well and Lee couldn't help thinking that she was more contented with her elder son than with Phillip. Brad was much kinder to her and more considerate in every way and yet she had sent him away because she feared for her husband's health. She must have thought a great deal of her husband. It may have been that her illness had been caused by regret over sending Brad away added to other worries. Lee felt she was quite recovered from whatever it was that caused her to slip into unconsciousness.

Brad was expecting them to stay with

him for several months and was making all sorts of plans for them to see other regions in Brazil. Lee would have liked to see the Mighty Amazon about which Brad had spoken before they arrived here, but he surprised her by telling her it involved a journey of four thousand miles from Rio and back. Brad said he would take them but his mother said she didn't want to go into the jungle regions. He assured her that by air they could do the journey and see quite a lot in a few days, but she said, 'You take Lee and leave me here. I shan't mind.'

So Brad promised that he would take Lee before they returned home. She was beginning to get used to being escorted by Brad. When his brother had taken her anywhere he had always made her feel he was doing her a favour by allowing her to accompany him, but Brad was the opposite. He made her feel *she* was doing *him* a favour and he liked to introduce her to his friends, not as his mother's secretary as Phillip used to, but as a friend, and his friends were different from Phillip's too. He had many Brazilian friends and they were nice to know, and they all welcomed Lee warmly.

Not all of Brad's friends lived in smart houses or apartments. Some lived in matchbox houses pressed together between the hillsides and with Brad Lee saw the shanty town clinging precariously to the Botafogo flank of Donna Marta. These names were given to her by Brad and she made especial notes of them so that she could quote them for Mrs Palmerston when she was making notes of all she could learn about Rio. It was amazing how the houses managed to stay put. They were perched on the steep slopes and at one point there was a granite quarry eating into the hillside and Lee was afraid for the safety of the children playing above it. People in these shacks had no water, no electricity, no plumbing. They did have magnificent views from their homes but those living at the top had an eight hundred foot climb to reach their houses.

Brad took Lee to get a closer look at Christ the Redeemer, but she preferred the view of it from the sea where it looked much more impressive. After climbing the final bit of the Corcovado the great statue created by the sculptor Landowski and intended to celebrate the hundredth anniversary of the Brazilian Independence as a kingdom, they saw it was a hundred-foot mass of reinforced concrete which Lee said was most disappointing. 'It looks magnificent down below, but not very marvellous close to.'

'Most people are disappointed when they get a closer view of it,' said Brad, 'but you must admit that the view from here is great, don't you agree?'

And she did agree as they looked down on the lower slopes on to delightful houses some of which had swimming pools to be seen quite clearly. 'It's like a picture post card,' she remarked.

They had made this journey on their own and Lee felt she was in a magical world. Brad took her into an old hotel which had an uninterrupted view to the Atlantic beaches fifteen hundred feet below. The food was good and Brad tempted Lee to try the Brazilian beer. She was so thirsty she did and found it deliciously cool. The food was good and the air intoxicating.

Many times Brad had seemed drawn close to Lee and on this occasion she felt they were drawn closer still. In such an atmosphere they couldn't fail to be light-hearted and happy and as they climbed to the heights he held her hand possessively.

When they left the restaurant after their delightful meal they saw that a feeble looking iron rail was all that stood between them and the sheer drop to the beach far below so Brad not only held her hand possessively then, he clung to her tightly as parents did with their children.

Finding herself leaning on him for

safety she could feel the strong beat of his heart and wondered if he could feel hers as his hands were clasped around her waist from behind. She liked to feel his strong fingers holding her. And then he turned her around so that he could kiss her. She had had numerous light kisses, quite brotherly ones, from him but this one was not like that at all. It was breathtaking. She was already standing at a great height, but she seemed to soar higher and higher into the clouds and she didn't want him to stop kissing her.

'I knew I would have to do that sooner or later,' he said, smiling at her afterwards, and she could have told him that she had been waiting for him to do so, and she hoped it had thrilled him as it had done her.

'How would you like to spend part of your life out here in Brazil with me?' he asked.

Her heart stood still. It would be wonderful to live anywhere with him but did he mean as his wife or just as a friend as she was now? She didn't like to ask him what his intentions were.

'Well, I've certainly been happy for the short time I've been here,' she said, evading his question.

'I feel I am torn between Brazil and England,' he said. 'Especially since I've been back home for a time. It is said that Brazil grows on you and I have settled down well. There are excellent opportunities here. I've got a finger in a good many pies and am doing quite well for myself. I never realised it could be so easy to get rich, and I realise there are problems in England at the present time. Yet, even so, I find myself longing to be back there at times.'

'I have heard it said that if you have lived in two countries you can't be contented in either for you are always yearning to go back to the other.'

'Perhaps, but in these days of high speed travel you can always satisfy a yearning by going back to the other country for a stay of a few weeks. Going back to England made me realise that my home is really there, and yet I'd be a fool to give up my connections here so it would mean travelling between the two.'

'Perhaps it's as well that you have your interests here as you and Phillip don't hit it off that well together. You could let him run the estate at home but at the same time, keep an eye on the way things are going.'

'I only wish I had more confidence in him,' said Brad. 'But you never know. He might change.'

They both stood looking down from the great height but not actually seeing the scenery. Brad drew Lee close to his side and kissed her again. 'It's been fine having you out here with me, Lee,' he said. 'Do you think you could be happy spending part of your life out here?'

That would depend on whether he wanted her to spend it as his wife, she told herself. Was he proposing to her? Surely he wouldn't suggest her spending part of every year out here with him unless she was married to him. And then she remembered Iris, Phillip's girl. He had brought her out here with him and where was she now? Married to someone else. She didn't want to be treated like that.

She turned away ready to start the downward trek. 'I'd have to see,' she said, lightly.

Brad became rather reserved after that and Lee felt mad for spoiling what had been a very intimate moment. And yet she wasn't going to agree to an affair with Brad just when he felt he wanted her. Spending part of the year out here with him didn't mean marriage, did it? If he wanted her to share all her time with him, partly here and the rest in England as his wife it would be marvellous. Why didn't he say whether he meant marriage or not? She became quiet, too, and what had promised to be a wonderful day, the most wonderful of her life, petered out and they returned home, both in a subdued frame of mind.

Having had Phillip's girl Iris on her

mind quite a lot after Brad's suggestion that Lee spent part of the year out here with him it was a surprise to meet her at a party a few days later. Mrs Palmerston was with her and Brad and as soon as she saw her she gave Lee's hand a squeeze. 'Goodness!' she said. 'There's Iris who was once Phillip's girl.'

Lee was naturally eager to see what sort of girl she was. What kind of girl Phillip really went for. She was a shortish girl, pretty, and well-dressed, wearing quite a lot of jewellery, but there was something about her that Lee didn't like. Watching her mix with the people there and talking away, Lee had the feeling that she was acting a part and that her smile was not genuine.

When she saw Brad her smile faded. She gave him a look that could have been called insolent, and then she pointedly cut him dead and turned to speak to someone else.

Lee looked at Brad who seemed merely amused. Later, when he was busily talking to someone and Mrs Palmerston was also engaged in conversation with an older member at the party, Iris came up to Lee and said, 'Are you with Brad or Mrs Palmerston?'

'Brad's mother is spending a holiday with her son and she invited me to come along, too,' said Lee.

'Do you know him very well?' asked Iris.

'No. I happen to work for his mother.'

'Oh,' said Iris. 'I was going to say you'd get nowhere with Brad. He's had no end of girls but he's not the marrying type.'

'So I gather,' said Lee, trying to appear unconcerned. She wondered how far the affair had gone between Iris and Brad. She couldn't imagine that she was Brad's type at all, but there was no accounting for taste. Phillip had cared for her a lot; it had taken him a long time to get over her, he'd said. Perhaps she gave herself generously to Brad only to be dropped when he was tired of her. And maybe this had happened several times. Lee was glad to be warned about him.

Iris was joined by a middle-aged, balding man who was perspiring freely, and Lee was horrified to discover that he was her husband. How could a young girl like Iris marry a man like that? He wasn't much to look at and was more than old enough to be her father.

Of course he had to be wealthy, Lee was in no doubt about that, because Iris didn't look at him with any affection in her eyes. She had been Phillip's girl and when Brad let her down she was sure Phillip would have taken her back again. He had told Lee that Iris was the only girl he had ever wanted to marry. But of course, Phillip was not in a position to give her the good things in life so that was probably the reason she didn't get in touch with him again.

Brad came along and asked her to dance with him and as they danced he spoke to her softly. 'What was the beautiful Iris telling you?' he asked.

'She was telling me not to trust you,' said Lee. 'I told her I was here with your mother on holiday and I let her see that you mean nothing to me.'

His eyes went hard. 'Is that true?'

'Is what true?' she asked, innocently.

'That I mean nothing to you?'

'Of course it is,' she said.

He finished the dance with her without saying another word and she could see he was terribly angry with her. But his anger didn't make him react in the way Phillip's did. She couldn't see that he should be angry with her just because she'd told him he meant nothing to her. She couldn't mean anything to him, after all, for hadn't he tried to get her married off to his brother?

His anger continued. He didn't offer to take her out again unless his mother was accompanying them. Lee could see that his mother was puzzled. She watched the pair of them. It was no use pretending nothing had changed because it had. They hardly spoke to each other and it wasn't giving them any satisfaction to ignore each other for they both looked miserable.

When his mother said perhaps it was time they returned to England, Lee thought perhaps it was a good idea though she couldn't bear the thought of leaving Brad even though they were not friends any more.

Brad said it was stupid to talk of going back to England so soon. 'You've only just arrived,' he told his mother.

'I suggested it because you look fed up at times, Brad, and I thought it might be restricting for you having your mother staying here with you. I daresay you entertain your own friends more when you're on your own.'

Probably had girls to stay with him, thought Lee, whom he wouldn't invite while his mother was here and that could explain why he had been glad of her own company for a time. He was missing his usual girl friends and the pleasure they gave him.

'There's no one I would rather have than you, Mother,' he said, 'so you can stop your worrying.'

He looked at Lee and she nearly offered to go back to England on her own for it was quite obvious that her presence here gave him no pleasure. But he wouldn't agree to that, she felt sure, because she was company for his mother while he was at work.

She hated not being on that lovely friendly basis they had known, but it was better to keep things as they were than to go on thinking more and more of him when he never took any girl seriously.

'Do you want to go back to England?' he asked, shortly.

'It's up to your mother,' she said, miserably. 'If you want me to go I will, or if you want me to stay on with your mother, I will.'

'I asked if you wanted to go home?' he repeated.

She met his eyes which were cold and unfriendly and she could have wept.

She was miserable, terribly unhappy, but she didn't want to leave him so she said, 'I'd like to stay if your mother decides to stay on.'

'Well, that's settled,' he said. 'You go when my mother goes and you're not going yet, Mother. There are a lot more places I want you to see before you return to England.'

Mrs Palmerston looked at Lee as if to say he was a bossy person, but she accepted his decision and her employee didn't know whether to be glad or not. It was hell being treated so coldly by Brad, and it would be even greater hell to have to go and leave him and perhaps never see him again.

9

A week later they had to leave Rio de Janeiro after all, for Brad received a phone call informing him that Phillip had had a serious car accident and was in the hospital.

His mother was so shocked they were afraid.

'Mother, they said he was seriously injured, not critically,' said Brad. 'You hear of people being seriously hurt in car crashes and in a few weeks they are back to normal these days.'

But he couldn't calm her down. She was shaking with nerves. He arranged the flight home and Lee took care of the packing because her employer was too shocked to do anything. She couldn't wait to get home to her son. It was a great blessing to be able to fly from one side of the world to the other in a matter of hours instead of days or weeks, but it was still a long tiring journey from Rio and Mrs Palmerston was exhausted when they landed back in England.

Brad lost no time in hiring a car to take them home as quickly as possible and then he took his mother to the hospital. No matter how tired she was she couldn't be persuaded to let him go alone to the hospital; she insisted on going with him.

Lee stayed behind. She would be the last person Phillip would want to see. But she was anxious to know how he was. It was awful to think that he might have injuries from which he might never recover or be disabled if he did.

When Brad and his mother returned after what seemed an eternity they told Lee he had facial injuries which could be attended to later so that they would hardly see a scar, and more serious, leg injuries. They had been told that he was lucky to have got away without anything worse for his car was a complete wreck.

Brad didn't tell Lee but Mrs Palmerston did later, that Phillip had been drinking and was the cause of the accident which injured two other people in the car he ran into. That shocked Lee.

'So he'll have to face a charge of driving under the influence?'

'Yes,' said his mother, and dissolved into tears.

Brad came upon Lee trying to comfort Mrs Palmerston. 'I blame myself,' he said. 'I shouldn't have agreed to let him have all that money. Apparently he's been living it up while we've been away.'

'I shouldn't have left him,' sobbed his mother.

'Goodness Mother!' exclaimed Brad. 'Phillip's a man. He's nearly thirty. You can't be behind him all his life.'

Lee noticed that they were both blaming themselves for Phillip's accident when he himself was to blame and no one else.

As the days went on she gathered that he was a difficult patient and plans were being made to bring him home to be cared for by a private nurse. He didn't want to stay in the hospital any longer.

While Brad and his mother were busy going backwards and forwards to visit Phillip, Lee busied herself in the study. They discovered that Phillip had left everything in a shambles. No book-keeping had been done since Lee had left and if Phillip had required anything he had apparently searched through loads of papers instead of going to the appropriate file and it could be seen that he had thrown bills and correspondence down anywhere in a temper when he hadn't been able to find what he wanted, and yet she had left everything straightforward for him, and explained where he would find everything he wanted. It was a simple thing, surely, to trace a bill or a contract when it was filed away neatly in alphabetical order. He was hopeless not only at running the estate, but in keeping the accounts in order.

Everything was arranged for his comfort when they had him home. A downstairs room with french windows opening out on to the gardens was made into a bed-sitting room for him. Brad installed a television set with remote control and a young nurse was engaged to come and attend to him just as if he were still in the hospital.

Brad would be available if Phillip required anything during the night. Lee went in to see Phillip when he was installed in the room made available for him. She had expected him to snub her but he was quite amiable considering that he had been giving everyone a bad time.

The young nurse, who said 'Call me Jenny', was a person who stood no nonsense. Phillip obeyed her every instruction if he obeyed no one else. She was at his beck and call, Lee noticed, but it didn't seem to bother her. It was her job to look after him.

Lee wondered that he had been allowed out of the hospital for his face was a sight and one arm and both legs were in plaster. Lee had a horrible feeling she would burst into laughter when she first saw him for he looked as if he had been got up to take one of those comedy parts where an actor is shown from head to foot in plaster.

The arm was a straightforward break, and one of his legs had seemed as if it would cause little trouble once it had mended, but his right leg was giving cause for concern for the fractures had been pretty serious. It was a matter of time to see how well the bones would knit together. And Phillip hadn't wanted to spend that time in the hospital. There would have to be frequent visits backwards and forwards, of course, but Phillip was happier being at home in between the visits and Brad and his mother didn't mind what trouble they went to for him.

Although it had taken hours for Lee

to clear up the mess in the study, Brad had made no nasty comments about the chaos. He had simply stood and looked at it all. And then the days began to fall into routine again. Mrs Palmerston had got over the initial shock of knowing that her son had been injured and began to console herself because he was not in a critical condition though it was not yet known whether he would ever walk properly again.

His mother's greatest worry now was the knowledge that Phillip would be charged with drunken driving. Fortunately the other couple injured were recovering with no serious injuries or Phillip might have found himself on a manslaughter charge.

Brad seemed very quiet and Lee didn't know whether he was worried more over the state of affairs in England or about his business concern in Brazil. Perhaps he was beginning to wish he hadn't got in touch with his family again, and yet that was unfair, for he couldn't have done more for his mother or Phillip.

He was friendly towards herself, but nothing more. He had thanked her for being such a help to his mother when she had been so upset. But there were no intimate little talks as there had been in the past and she knew that if he had been going to show any signs of caring for her at all she had stifled them when she told him he meant nothing to her. He was proud and wouldn't risk again the mistake of thinking she might be interested in him. Yet if he took girls casually and dropped them just as casually as Iris had suggested it couldn't bother him very much if one girl had failed to fall for his charms.

Strangely enough Phillip began to show an affection towards the young nurse who bossed him around all the time making him do exercises even though he was encased in plaster, and standing no nonsense from him at all. Phillip, who had always considered himself above taking orders from any-one, and believed he should be the one to give them, meekly obeyed this slip of a girl and was bad-tempered when she left him at the end of the day.

When they were all gathered in his room one evening after Jenny had left he suggested they made arrangements for her to live in instead of having to leave every day to go home. 'We have plenty of room to accommodate her,' he said.

'She can have my room,' said Lee, immediately. 'I'll go home at the end of the day. I don't live far away.'

'There's no need for that, Lee,' said Mrs Palmerston, quickly. 'We can easily prepare a room for Jenny if she agrees to stay.'

Brad smirked at Phillip. 'You've fallen for that bossy young nurse,' he accused.

Phillip growled. 'You keep your eyes off her.'

'Oh, come off it, Phillip,' said Brad. 'You like to let everyone believe I stole

Iris from you and you know I did you a favour when I took her off to South America with me.'

Phillip grinned sheepishly. 'I'll admit that now,' he said, 'but I was furious when she went off with you after I'd spent a fortune on her.'

'I didn't ask her to come with me,' said Brad. 'She invited herself and I knew I'd be doing you a good turn if I took her away from you. When she asked if she could come with me I told her straight she would have to pay her own fare but in actual fact the Palmerstons paid it because I happen to know that she sold some of the jewellery you gave her to buy her ticket.'

Again Phillip looked sheepish. 'So you knew she ruined me? And it was I, Mother, who owed all that money to Lesters for jewellery. I let you and Dad believe it was Brad who'd run up those debts to buy gifts for all the girls he knew.'

Lee listened in amazement to Phillip.

He had allowed her to believe that Brad was a rotter when in actual fact it was he who had been a rotter. Brad didn't seem to bear any malice towards his brother and his mother didn't say a lot so Lee assumed that she had had her suspicions about Phillip all along.

And Lee had allowed Iris to blacken Brad's character, too, when the girl had no doubt been spiteful because she hadn't been able to get anywhere with Brad.

Seeing that Phillip was not annoyed at the mention of Iris now encouraged Brad to continue talking about her. 'I knew she told you she was leaving with me and I guessed you'd believe it, but I made it quite clear to her from the start that there was nothing doing. I'd heard so much about her from other men, the way she had played one against the other, getting as much as she could out of them. You should see the man she's married, shouldn't he, Lee? He's absolutely rolling in money and that's the reason she went for him. He's a detestable man in my opinion, but she deserves him. I can't believe it's given her any happiness to be tied to him.'

'I thought her smile seemed very false,' said Lee, and told herself what a fool she'd been to listen to her. She wasn't happy herself and didn't want anyone else to be either.

Lee felt upset and angry that Phillip's and Iris had given her the wrong impression of Brad. It wasn't fair. People couldn't be blamed for believing what they were told.

It was surprising that Phillip was confessing to his own faults of the past. His accident must have changed him, but it was rather late in the day now because Lee had given Brad the brush off and he wasn't making any attempt to get round her at all.

As the days passed it became even more obvious that Jenny was having a great effect on Phillip. It seemed that he would do anything for her. But then she had told him he must think himself lucky he was alive and also the occupants of the other car. 'You have a lot to be thankful for,' she continually rubbed it in whenever he was inclined to feel sorry for himself.

It amazed Lee to see how humble he was when Jenny snapped at him and told him to pull himself together and count his blessings. She was the right sort of person to deal with him.

Jenny had agreed to settle in the Palmerstons' home so that she could be with him constantly and she didn't seem to mind at all that he monopolised all her time which proved, either that she was extremely dedicated to her work, or that she was extremely fond of Phillip. It seemed to Lee and the others that she was fond of him and Lee hoped it would lead to something good for Phillip.

Brad must have spent a fortune in phone calls to Brazil and he was often short-tempered which was unusual for him.

'If you are anxious to get back to your work, Brad,' said his mother,

'We ought to think about getting a manager in.'

'I have colleagues who can carry on for some time in my absence,' said Brad. 'I'm not going back until Phillip's definitely on the mend.'

He worked hard out of doors. It didn't seem that he could sit about doing nothing; he just had to be active. He could be seen spraying the fields and Lee knew that Phillip usually employed someone to do that job. He checked the fences, kept an eye on the cattle, called in the vet if he was doubtful about any animal. They had odd job men working about the estate but it seemed Brad worked harder than any of them, worked himself almost to a standstill. He said he didn't believe in paying someone to do jobs he was capable of doing himself with nothing more important to do.

Mrs Palmerston was getting on extremely well with Jenny and Lee hadn't had a break to go home for a long time so she asked if it would be okay to spend a few days with her family.

'By all means,' said Mrs Palmerston. 'You don't need to ask for permission, Lee. You just tell us when you want to go.'

Lee hoped that by getting away from the Palmerstons she would be able to get Brad out of her system. It wouldn't affect him whether she was there or not and it seemed that now Mrs Palmerston had Jenny to depend on she wouldn't miss her either. The thought that no one would miss her very much depressed Lee and she felt near to tears. It wasn't often that she indulged in self pity like that, but she was feeling in the depths of misery because Brad didn't like her any more.

At home with her family she was able to sit and think quietly knowing that Brad's eyes were not upon her. She had often caught him watching her with a deep brooding sort of expression in his eyes.

It was strange that she had wanted to get away from his presence and yet away from him she thought of him even more than when he was around. The man was an obsession. He haunted her waking and sleeping. She thought so much of that time when he had kissed her on the Corcovado, given her her first really passionate kiss, that she dreamt about it. Sometimes they were close to that fragile looking rail in her dreams and both of them went plunging down those fifteen hundred feet and she would wake with a start to spend more hours of sleeplessness.

The deep tan which she had acquired in Rio had hidden the look of strain at first, but as it began to fade people noticed that her face had become thinner and her eyes seemed too large. She became tired of people asking her if she was feeling all right and wanted to go away and hide where no one could ask questions and wonder why she was looking so tragic.

Brad had been so reserved and kept

his distance so much since she had told him he meant nothing to her that he hadn't given her any encouragement to tell him that she didn't mean it. Just the slightest bit of kindness from him would encourage her to speak to him, tell him what Iris had said, and let him know that she did care about him. More than anything in the world.

Her mother was most concerned about her and asked if she was feeling well.

'Do you think it did you any good going off to that hot country, Lee?' she asked. 'I know you were wonderfully tanned when you first came back but I looked at your eyes and didn't think you were as well as you looked. Now the tan's almost gone you definitely look under the weather.'

'And you've lost a lot of weight, too,' said her father. 'I was telling your mother how thin you are.'

'It could have been the heat, Dad,' said Lee. 'It was very hot and humid.'

'It wouldn't suit me then,' said her

mother. 'I can't stand too much heat though I will say that it would be nice if we could have some warmer summers and more sunshine than we've been having.'

Lee tried to appear on top of the world to stop them worrying and asking too many questions. She told them about the places she had visited while she'd been in Rio. 'Brad was going to take me into the Amazon forests before we left but of course we had to come back earlier because of Phillip's accident.'

'Yes, we heard about that,' said her mother. 'People who saw the accident were furious when they knew the driver of the car which ploughed into the other had been drinking. They said it was a terrible crash and a wonder no one was killed.'

'I think Phillip knows he has to thank his lucky stars. It seems to have changed him. Brought him down to earth a bit. His case will be heard shortly and he'll lose his licence for a time, I suppose, and will be heavily fined, but he could have been on a manslaughter charge and I think he realises that. His mother is always expressing her relief that he didn't kill anyone.'

'I expect it has taught him a good lesson,' said her mother.

Lee had intended to buy presents for all of her family while she'd been abroad but they understood that they had had to leave in a hurry because of Phillip's accident.

She was like a fish out of water at home with nothing to do. There were times when she told herself she would be wise to get herself a job away from the Palmerstons so that she could forget Brad, but even as she thought about it she knew that she wouldn't. While there was a chance of seeing him she would continue to do so although she was torturing herself wanting to be near him when he took so little notice of her.

To pass the time away she went

shopping with her mother and she bought her a present to make up for not buying her one while she was away. It was a really smart leather handbag, rather pricey, but Lee wanted to treat her and she was very thrilled with it. 'Oh, our Lee!' she cried. 'What a lot of money to spend on a present for me and it's not my birthday or anything.'

It pleased Lee to see her mother with an expensive handbag similar to the type Mrs Palmerston took for granted.

She helped her with the housework, took her in her Mini to visit relatives who had been neglected. It wasn't a very satisfactory way to spend her break away from work, but then she'd had a good holiday in Rio de Janeiro. As the days went by she became conscious more than she'd ever been in her life that she wasn't really necessary to anyone's happiness. Her mother enjoyed her company, loved having her at home, but carried on quite well when she was not at home. Mrs Palmerston now wouldn't rely on her so much for there was Jenny to chatter to. No one really wanted Lee and she felt very sorry for herself. She supposed she ought to spend more time at home, go out and meet young people as she used to and find herself a nice young fellow to settle down with. That was what she ought to do.

After a week at home she decided she would go back to work. There was always something waiting for her to do. Now that Phillip's mother had got over the shock she was settling down to her writing once more and perhaps she was waiting for Lee to type out some articles for her. She hoped so. It was nice to feel useful.

As she drove her Mini on to the forecourt of her employer's home she found her heart pounding away at the thought of seeing Brad again. She looked across the fields and imagined she saw him in the distance talking to someone. That was a relief. She could at least enter the house feeling cool, calm and collected.

Mrs Palmerston made no secret of the fact that she was glad to see her. Jenny greeted her warmly and Lee felt that even Phillip was more friendly than usual. As soon as she was settled in she went into the study to see how much work had piled up while she'd been away. No one else did any book-keeping here. It wasn't a full-time job keeping the accounts for the estate but the work soon accumulated if it wasn't kept up to date.

Letters had been opened, in some cases Brad had written comments on them for Lee's attention. Perhaps querying a price, or asking to try and get an earlier delivery date for certain commodities. He wasn't so bad as Phillip for messing everything up in the study, but he left letters piled up for her attention and Lee was glad because it justified her presence here. She wouldn't feel she earned her wages if she didn't find plenty of work to do.

There was an article waiting to be

typed and Lee settled down contentedly to work. There was enough to keep her going here for a day or two and there was nothing like work for making her forget herself.

She was so busy she didn't notice the door open and when she heard Brad's voice she nearly jumped out of her skin.

'So you're back, Lee,' he said, giving her such a nice smile it turned her heart over.

'Hello, Brad,' she smiled in return. 'I didn't hear you come.'

'Mother said you'd arrived and I thought I'd just come and explain some of those notes I've put here and there.'

'I've looked through them,' she said, 'and I think I understand all you want me to do.'

'That's good. It's nice to see you back again,' he said. 'We've missed you.'

He was looking at her as if he was really feasting his eyes on her. Her dark hair fitted like a velvety silk cap and she was wearing a cool looking cream and green dress which fitted her slim figure to perfection.

'Have you enjoyed your little break?'

'Yes, thanks,' she said, looking down at the papers on her desk after taking a quick look at him. He was dressed in casual clothes but looked as handsome as ever. His tan was too deep to be fading yet. She found she was terribly shy. It had been a long time since he'd shown such friendliness towards her.

'Been seeing your boy friend?' he asked, picking up a paper weight and weighing it in his hands.

'I haven't a boy friend,' she said. 'Not a particular one.'

'It's time you did have someone,' he said, teasing her.

'What about you,' she retorted. 'You're a lot older than I am.'

'No one will have me,' he said, pretending to look sorry for himself.

'What a shame,' she smiled, as she rose to get a folder.

As she moved closer to him to reach for the folder she wanted, he caught her wrist and drew her towards him. 'I've been thinking about you all the time you've been away,' he said.

She nearly blurted out that she had been thinking of him, too; instead she kept her eyes down, afraid to look at him in case she should reveal her feelings to him.

'Have you been thinking about me, just a little?' he asked, coaxingly.

'No, I haven't,' she lied.

'Not just a little? Do you ever think, Lee, about that time we kissed on the Corcovado by the huge statue?'

'Sometimes,' she murmured, but if she was truthful she would have told him that she thought about it all the time. The fact that he was so close to her, holding on to her, reminding her of that wonderful moment was too much for her. Suddenly she gave a little sob, and then she was reduced to uncontrollable tears. She had been so unhappy for weeks and now it all came rushing out, all the misery that had been bottled up within her. She wouldn't have behaved like this if he hadn't been so nice to her. That was her undoing.

'Lee!' he cried, in concern. 'What is it? What have I said to upset you so much? Has something awful happened while you've been away?'

'No, no,' she mumbled, and her body shook with her crying. He held her tight, patting her, murmuring to her, saying soothing words to try and calm her. 'Tell me what's wrong,' he pleaded, moving his hand gently up and down her back, in an attempt to comfort her.

Could she confess that she loved him? Would it embarrass him if she did? Hot tears kept streaming down her face and now that they'd started she couldn't stop them and she felt awful.

'What must you think of me?' she cried.

'Don't worry about what I'm thinking. Lee, you're drowning me in tears,' he said, huskily. 'You must tell me what's the matter. How can I help you if I don't know what's wrong?'

'I'm sorry,' she sobbed, 'I can't stop it.'

'Shall I fetch my mother?'

'No, no,' she said in alarm. 'She's got enough to trouble her.'

'But you've comforted her when she's been upset.'

'I shall be all right, don't worry.' She held her hand tightly across her mouth to stop it from trembling. 'You must think me an awful idiot. Men don't like girls who cry, do they?'

'I don't think you're an idiot and I don't dislike girls who cry if they've something to cry over. Tears are very often a safety valve. It does us good to have a good cry. I suppose we should do it more often,' he said, smiling gently at her, 'instead of keeping things bottled up inside.'

'I'm all right now,' she said, sniffing

and giving him a watery smile.

He sat her down. 'Just calm down while I fetch you a drink and you're going to tell me what this is all about,' he said, firmly.

10

Brad left Lee to complete mopping up operations while he went for some coffee which he knew she preferred to tea. She sniffed and blew her nose and did her best to get herself under control. What an awful thing to do, to break down like that in front of him! She felt like running away, but he would come after her, she felt sure.

When he returned he gave her a keen look as he poured the coffee and handed her a cup and then poured one for himself. She couldn't look at him, just sipped her coffee in silence after thanking him for it, and he sat in silence, too, drinking his.

After a bit she looked at him rather shamefaced and he said, 'What is it that's upsetting you like that?'

She didn't answer and he said, 'Been fiddling the accounts, or made a terrible blunder or something?' He was smiling and when she still didn't tell him he went on, 'Or did you have a special boy friend and he's chucked you?'

'No,' she said, smiling in spite of herself. 'Nothing like that.'

'Not going to tell me?'

She shook her head and he said, 'I'd like to help you but I can't if you don't tell me what's wrong. Come on. You can tell Brad, can't you?'

'Oh, it was something I said to you when we were in Rio,' she said, turning her face away from him.

He frowned. 'Something you said all that time ago and you're still worrying over it?'

She coloured and looked confused. 'It may not be important to you,' she went on, 'but I lied to you.'

His eyes narrowed. 'When was that?'

'It was when you asked me if you meant anything to me and I said you didn't.'

He sat perfectly still for a moment then he got up and put his coffee cup down. He took her cup, put it down and then drew her to her feet and said, 'Now, tell me that again.'

'I lied to you.'

He was looking at her incredulously. 'That means I did mean something to you?'

'Yes.'

'And still do?'

She tried to turn away from him, feeling dreadful in case he didn't want to hear such a thing but he held her firmly and made her look at him. 'You put us both in hell for weeks for no reason?'

'It was what Iris said,' she told him, miserably.

'Ahhhh! I should have known. And what did Iris say?'

'She said you'd had lots of girls and you just casually dropped them when you tired of them.'

He gave a short laugh. 'So you'd believe her before me?'

'I thought she knew you better than I did. She was warning me not to let myself be carried away by you. And Phillip told me not to trust you.'

'Charming,' he said, coldly.

'You did try to get me married off to Phillip,' she accused. 'You offered him all that money so that he could marry me.'

'I told you I would explain about that,' he said. 'But the most important thing now is that you do like me a little, don't you?'

She nodded and he said, 'More than a little?'

She hid her face against his chest and he held her tight. 'Little idiot,' he murmured. He held her for a moment then released her and moved away. She wondered what she had done now, but he went to lock the door and she felt her pulses racing. Locking the door meant only one thing. And it did. He came and took her in his arms and then she was being kissed, savagely.

'Brad!' she protested, 'that hurt.'

And yet his kiss didn't upset her as Phillip's savage kisses had done.

Brad gave a deep sigh. 'You deserve that for what you've put me through,' he said, and then he drew her close again to give her a more tender kiss which made her bones melt and she could hardly support herself. She had to lean upon him.

'Brad!' she breathed.

'Was that better?' he asked, with a tender look in his eyes.

'Oh, yes, much better.'

And of course he wasn't satisfied with one kiss. He had to keep repeating the performance and Lee didn't mind at all.

'I wanted to tell you,' she said, when she got her breath back, 'that I would come and stay with you in Rio whenever you wanted me to, but I wouldn't agree right away because I couldn't agree to anything like that without giving it a lot of thought.'

He pushed her away from him so that he could look deeply into her eyes. 'Did you think I asked you if you would mind staying with me in

Rio for parts of the year just to have an affair?' he asked, incredulously.

'I did,' she said, looking him in the eye. 'You didn't give me the impression that you wanted anything else. You just asked me if I would be happy spending part of my life out there with you.'

'It seems you have a wonderful opinion of me,' he said, his mouth grim. 'You think I'd have a girl, take all I want from her and then I'd casually drop her.'

'I was only going on what people told me about you.'

'What sort of person are you anyway, that you would agree to have an affair with a man like that? What would your parents think, and my mother?'

Lee's face flushed angrily. 'You don't consider what people will think when you're in love,' she said.

He stared at her and then he laughed. 'Say that again,' he cried. 'It's great to hear you say it. You're in love. With me?'

'Why should I say it again?' she

snapped. 'You haven't told me you love me, have you?'

'Yes, I have. I told you when I asked you to stay with me in Rio for parts of the year. The other parts you would be with me in England as my wife, you silly nitwit. Don't you understand that I'll be travelling backwards and forwards from one country to another looking after business affairs? That's the sort of life I'll be leading and I wondered if you'd mind. That's why I asked if you could spend part of your life with me in Rio. I felt you would agree after that lovely day we spent together and that wonderful kiss.'

'You didn't make it clear that you loved me,' she said, 'and knowing your reputation it was likely that I should misunderstand you.'

'My reputation! I'll have you know that I haven't had lots of girls in the way you seem to believe. I've *known* lots of girls, which is a different thing altogether. For the past few years I've been very unsettled. It's taken me two years to get myself sorted out in Brazil. I've got something to offer a wife now. And the very first time I saw you on horseback with Phillip I fell like a ton of bricks. I envied Phillip because I thought you belonged to him. It seemed as if you did when you both came towards me, and whatever Phillip may have said about me, I would not have gone out of my way to steal you from him if you'd had an understanding between you.'

'There's some explaining to do there,' she cried. 'You knew very well he'd upset me and yet you told him he could have a large amount of money from you so that he'd be in a position to marry me. Why did you do that?'

'Because I was sure you wouldn't accept him. But I wanted him and mother to know that I wasn't going to step in and try to win you until you had made it clear that you had no intention of marrying him with or without money.'

'Supposing I'd been tempted by the

money and accepted him?'

'Then you wouldn't have been the girl I thought you were.'

'Why didn't you explain that to me?'

'I didn't know how you felt about me, did I?'

'You didn't care that I was upset over Phillip's proposal because I felt you'd tried to push me into marrying him?'

'I did. I cared very much. I asked you to come to Rio with mother. You should have known how I felt when I invited you both to come with me.'

'How could I know if you didn't tell me?'

He laughed into her eyes. 'Why the devil are we arguing, darling?'

'I don't know,' she beamed, and suddenly put her arms up and around his neck. 'Oh, Brad, I love you so much. I can't believe that out of all the girls you've known you would fall for me.'

'Ah, you can't see yourself as I do,'

he smiled. 'You're lovely to look at and nice to know. You haven't time to put on an act to impress people, have you? You are always busy doing something and you're perfectly natural. I've been seeing you all the time you've been away this week, sitting at that desk, I've thought of these lovely, capable hands, typing on that machine, turning over these papers. I think I have everything about you clearly imprinted in my mind. You've bewitched me, my love. Don't ever doubt that I love you.'

Lee found herself being swept off her feet again and now she knew that Brad loved her she wasn't afraid to respond. She let her hands wander over his strong body, and allowed his hands to wander over hers and it was an indescribable joy.

Someone tried the study door and Brad stopped kissing her long enough to tell whoever it was to 'Go away'. She giggled, and let him carry on kissing her.

'Is there any reason why we shouldn't

be married within the next few weeks?' he asked.

'None at all,' she said, happily.

'Well, you'd better get cracking, my love, for I expect you'll want a white wedding and all the trimmings but don't take too long to arrange it all, will you?'

'Oh, Brad,' she murmured happily, imagining herself walking down the aisle to become his wife.

'You should have burst into tears sooner, sweetheart. We could have been married already if you hadn't been so silly. Telling me I didn't mean anything to you. Look at the time we've wasted.'

'You should have been more specific,' she told him, cheekily. 'You should have told me you had marriage in mind after you stole that first real kiss.'

'I didn't steal it,' he grinned. 'You were perfectly willing to let me have it. And you brazen creature, thinking of living in sin with me in Rio, without being married. Lee!'

She chuckled and he caught her close again. 'It's going to be great fun married to you,' she said, and she pictured him that day when they'd gone out horse-riding and he had been shouting out his joy as he went galloping across the fields.

'You did worry me when you cried so hard,' he said. 'I wondered what on earth was wrong. You were so unhappy and so was I, and look at us now.'

'If you've been as miserable as I have, Brad, I'm sorry.'

'And so you should be. I said we'd both been in hell and that's true, isn't it? But you have to know what it's like in hell to appreciate being in heaven all the more. I suppose we ought to go and break the news to mother. Whoever it was who tried that door might be imagining that I'm doing all sorts of wicked things to you.'

'Aren't you?' she grinned.

'Not half as wicked as I intend to be,' he laughed, pulling her with him as he unlocked the door.

'I ought to go and tidy myself up before going to see anyone,' she said, feeling that he had made her hot and bothered and all dishevelled.

'You look fine. You look as if you've just been thoroughly kissed,' he smirked, 'and if you value your virginity you'd better not be on your own with me too much until we're married or I won't be responsible for the consequences.'

'Cheeky,' she laughed, nudging him.

He had a wicked look in his eyes and she thought he was the most handsome man she'd ever seen. And he loved her.

Mrs Palmerston was in Phillip's room and Jenny was there, too, of course. Phillip's face was still a little unsightly and he was expecting to go into the hospital soon for plastic surgery. But he had only one leg in plaster now and had had a pin put in temporarily to help the bones knit. The doctors had more confidence now that it was going to mend satisfactorily. Jenny made sure that he constantly used the injured arm and the leg which was free of plaster so that the maximum use would be gained in time. There was really no need to have a nurse in constant attendance any more, but Phillip liked to have Jenny there, and she seemed happy enough.

When Lee and Brad entered they found all eyes upon them. There was really no need to tell them anything for their faces said it all. It had been obvious to everyone that there had been a coldness between them which had now disappeared and they were hand in hand smiling happily.

'I just came from the study,' said his mother, accusingly to Brad, 'and the door was locked.'

'Yes, I was living up to my reputation, Mother. I was making love to your secretary in your absence.'

She laughed. 'That's all right so long as your intentions are honourable.'

Brad smiled. 'I thought you were going to say my intentions were horrible,' and they all laughed. 'No, they're entirely honourable. Lee and I want to get married immediately.'

'If not sooner?' smiled Jenny, coming forward to congratulate them.

His mother seemed completely dazed by the news and Brad looked at her anxiously. 'Aren't you pleased, Mother?' he asked.

'Pleased? I'm absolutely over the moon, Brad. But I'd given up hope that you were ever going to ask her.'

'I asked her in Rio,' he said, 'but she didn't think I was the marrying kind.'

Mrs Palmerston hugged Lee and gave her a kiss. 'I'm so glad, dear. I said I'd love you for a daughter-in-law.'

'So it's all been a plot,' laughed Brad. 'You planned between you to get me hooked?'

'But you didn't seem to want to get caught,' beamed his mother. 'And don't think you are getting my secretary all for yourself. I need her, too.'

'I'm not sharing my wife with you.'

'Ignore him,' said Lee. 'I'll still do

your typing for you. And no one else wants to do the book-keeping so I reckon I'll still be doing that, too.'

Mrs Palmerston gave her son a kiss and Lee saw that there were tears in her eyes.

'I do envy you,' cried Jenny, giving her a hug.

'Because she's marrying Brad?' asked Phillip, quickly.

'No, you idiot. Because she's getting married.'

'I'll propose to you if ever I get this leg right again, and my face put right,' he consoled her.

'Do you think I wouldn't accept you as you are now?' she asked, smiling.

'I would be surprised if you ever accepted me,' he said. 'I've been like a bear with a sore head.'

'But your temper's improving all the time, love,' she said, smiling at him, fondly.

Phillip looked at Lee and Brad and said, 'Congratulations both. I'm very pleased for you, and now would you mind getting out so that I can propose to Jenny.'

'Charming,' said Brad, and then he patted his brother on the shoulder. 'Good luck, old man,' he said, and taking the hint they all left Phillip and Jenny on their own and it seemed there was little doubt that Jenny was going to accept his proposal, and it made Lee feel happier.

'Quick work on our kid's part,' grinned Brad, as they went off to the sitting room. 'I didn't think he could work that fast.'

'Don't be sarcastic,' laughed his mother. 'If Jenny accepts Phillip I'll be the happiest mother in the world for I'll have two delightful daughters-in-law.'

'Jenny's been a brick to Phillip,' said Brad. 'She's just the sort of girl he needs. I don't think he'd dare to go astray with a girl like that.'

'I think we ought to get in some champagne, Brad,' said his mother.

He put his arm around her. 'I'm glad something has happened to make you feel happy,' he smiled.

'If Jenny takes Phillip I'll be happier still,' she smiled. 'He needs someone of strong character that's why at one time I hoped he and Lee would marry. I couldn't have sent Phillip away from home, Brad. Goodness knows what sort of mess he'd have made of his life on his own.'

It was arranged that the marriage of Brad and Lee should take place within a month and her family was delighted about it. In one sense the month fled because there was so much to do arranging the wedding at such short notice, and in another sense it dragged, every day seeming an eternity until Lee could become Brad's wife.

There was no one more impatient than he was for the marriage to take place. They decided to go back to Rio for a few weeks after their marriage for Lee didn't object to his looking into his business affairs occasionally while they were over there on a honeymoon. He promised to take her to the Amazon forests this time, as they hadn't managed it before.

What they were going to do in the future was rather hazy. Phillip's case had come up in court and he had been heavily fined and his licence taken from him for a year. He couldn't have driven anyway, but Jenny could and she would be driving him wherever they went. She had accepted his proposal of marriage and after the court case had declared, 'I'll see that he never drinks and drives again,' and they were sure she would be successful.

They had talked over their future, Phillip and Jenny, and it transpired that Phillip would be quite willing to forgo his interest in the Palmerston estate completely. He had never been all that attached to the land as Brad had been. Jenny had suggested they bought a small hotel on the sea front and that appealed to Phillip, but they were waiting for his leg to heal properly, and then he had to have plastic surgery on his face.

'It may mean that I shall end up running the Palmerston estate after all, Lee,' said Brad. 'Nothing would give me greater pleasure, and yet I have enjoyed my interests in Brazil. If I sold out there I could buy all Phillip's share in the estate, I daresay, but I want him to be absolutely sure he knows what he's doing first. He might feel, when he's away from the estate that he wished he'd hung on to some of it, at least, so I shan't push anything.'

Lee listened to all Brad's plans without making any comments of her own.

'You don't offer any suggestions,' he said, curiously.

'I love your home and the estate, Brad. I enjoy doing the books, I like helping your mother. And you know how I enjoy horse-riding early in the morning. And then I enjoyed myself in Rio, there was so much to see and do. So you see I have no preference at all. It's up to you to do entirely as you wish and I'll be happy.'

He caught her close and gave her a kiss. 'How easily pleased you are,' he said.

'Easily pleased!' she exclaimed. 'Brad you've given me so much I just can't believe it.'

'There you are, enjoying things that it has cost me so little to give you. Most girls I've known have been far more ambitious. They have wanted jewellery, a fine home, and had a desire to be taken out to the most luxurious places.'

'Oh, surely not all girls are like that,' she said.

'Perhaps I've been unfortunate in the girls I have met but the majority of those I've known have expected far more from me than you do.'

'Perhaps they've been brought up to expect more,' she said. 'I was never spoilt as a child, except with love, which is the most important thing.'

'And you're going to be spoilt with love for the rest of your life,' he promised.

Lee believed that, for since he'd known that she loved him he hadn't been able to do enough for her. She knew he would have showered her with gifts and lovely clothes and all the things she hadn't been used to, but all she really wanted was his love. So long as she had that nothing else mattered. He left her in no doubt at all that she had his love, and she knew he would have hers as long as they both should live.

THE END